SINGLE DAD NEXT DOOR

CATHRYN FOX

COPYRIGHT

ISBN Print: 978-1-928056-87-4

ISBN ebook: 978-1-928056-88-1

RACHEL

When my bedroom door flies open and crashes hard against the paint-chipped wall, I groan. "Go away," I say, my voice muffled by my pillow. Not that my roommates will listen, even if they can hear me. Heck, I could scream at the top of my lungs and it wouldn't faze them, much less send them running back to their rooms —not when the view outside my window is that *hot*.

Seriously though, sharing a house with four college freshmans is not my idea of a good time, not when I'm a senior and working my ass off to get into law school. But when I left NYU two months before the start of my fourth year and transferred to Penn State at the last minute, this place was all I could find—and afford. Ultimately, Penn State is where I want to do my law degree after undergrad. I just ended up here sooner, rather than later.

Someone tugs at my pillow and I open one eye to see Becca hovering over me. "Come on, Rach, he just took his shirt off," she says. "You're going to want to see this."

Why oh why did my room have to come with the best view of the hot neighbor's driveway?

"Thank God for this heat wave." Sylvie, roommate number two, fans her face with her hand.

I groan and curl up into the fetal position. I just want one more minute in bed without every member of the house in my room. "I. Don't. Care." Well, that might be a lie. I like looking at the eye candy next door as well as they do, but after putting in a late night at Pizza Villa—I seriously have to find a new job—I need all the sleep I can get before class.

"Jesus, would you look at him," Becca says, her voice a breathy whisper as she peers out the window. "Talk about slurpalicious. I could seriously lick that from head to toe, and back up again."

"Leave," I say on a yawn.

Ignoring me, Sylvie squeals. "He's going back into his garage. Damned if he doesn't look as good going as he does coming."

"But I'd rather see him...*coming*," Becca says, and they start giggling.

"Seriously. Are you both twelve?"

"Shh, he's back," Becca says and swats her hand at me, like I'm an annoying fly that needs to be shooed away.

I shift on my bed, not to get a better look outside my window. No, moving has absolutely nothing at all to do with the shirtless mechanic turning my roommates into dim-witted moths. The *only* reason I'm getting up is to herd these girls from my room, and if I happen to get a glimpse of the hot, tattooed, badass daddy next door, well...then so be it.

I rub the blur from my eyes and toss my pillow at them. "Get away from my window, before he thinks it's me." They don't need to know that the hottie's bedroom window is also across from mine, and that late one night, he caught me staring into his room as he walked around in nothing but boxer shorts. Heck, if they knew that, they'd camp out for the rest of the school year, and that was so not happening.

"Ohmigod!" Sylvie leaps back. "I think he just saw me." She puts her hand over her mouth and starts to giggle. Footsteps pound down the hall, announcing the arrival of my other two roommates. I shake my head as they come bursting in.

Kill. Me. Now.

"Is he out there?" Val asks, her big blue eyes wide and hopeful.

"Yeah, but he saw me looking," Sylvie says. Despite that, she edges back around to sneak another look. Megan hurries across the room, and goes up on her toes to peer over Sylvie's shoulder, trying to catch a glimpse without getting caught.

"Do you really think he killed someone?" Megan asks.

"That's the rumor," Val protests, though her tone holds uncertain convictions.

"Then why isn't he in jail?"

"Maybe it was self-defense."

"He's such a badass."

"He's good with his little girl, though."

"Bad Boy Daddy, now that's hot."

"Do you think he'd spank me if I was bad?"

Unable to put up with their incessant chatter and giggles any longer, I point my finger toward the door. "Out. Now."

A chorus of grumbles ensues as they all sullenly walk to my door. Christ, I'm getting that lock fixed, even if I have to eat ramen noodles for the next month.

"God, you're such a grouch in the morning." Becca shoots me a wounded look over her shoulder.

"Doesn't even have to be the morning," Val adds with a hair toss.

"You need to get your nose out of a book once in a while," Megan says.

"What she needs is to get laid," Sylvie informs them all, but her solution to pretty much everything is sex. Problem is, this time Megan is nodding her head in sad agreement as she follows Sylvia out the door.

"I can hear you," I shout after them. I shake my head and my mussed hair falls over my shoulders. "I'm still right here." As I stand there, dressed only in my tank top and underwear, a warm breeze blows in and slides over my skin, a late reminder that I'd opened my window last night before crawling into bed exhausted. Great. Not only could the hot guy working on his car see my roommates drooling over him, he could *hear* them as well. *And* they just announced that I needed to get laid. How freaking mortifying. I stomp across the room and yell down the hall, "And don't bother to close my door on your way out." As usual my sarcasm is ignored.

I give the door a good slam, which helps improve my mood a little. With a deep breath, I turn around, not to see my hot neighbor, but to close my window. No way do I want him hearing anything else that goes on inside this place, or get the wrong idea that I might want him. I don't. Not in a million years.

I'm completely off guys, trying to keep a low profile. After my ex-boyfriend turned violent and abusive, threatening to kill me if I went to the police, I snuck away under the cover of darkness and put several states between us. His was big and hard like my neighbor, his muscles born from rough carpentry work. Last year, when he came to do repairs on the house I was sharing with friends, I was flattered that I was the object of his attention. At first he was doting and attentive, but as time went by, he became possessive and controlling, and I came to find out later, he'd had other charges against him from numerous other women.

Jesus, why am I such a bad judge of character when it comes to men. Oh, probably because my only role model had been a mean-assed, alcoholic father who drove my beautiful, caring mom to an early grave and me out of the house the second I turned eighteen.

If I try hard enough I can still smell the cheap perfume on his shirt when he stumbled in after a weekend-long drinking binge. God, how I hated those women he slept around with almost as much as I hated my Dad. Mom used to try to protect me from his disgusting behavior, but what hurt the most was how dragged Mom down, aging her pretty face far too early.

My heart squeezes as I think about her. She was a good woman, but was too afraid to leave. Running is hard. I get that now. Not that she really had anywhere to run. Our only other relative was my father's mother. She's still alive, living upstate Pennsylvania where my Dad was born. While she liked me well enough, when it came to Mom and Dad, she always took Dad's side. That's how it is with parents, I guess.

I lift my arms, place my hands on the frame, and lean in to give it a tug when the hottie slowly lifts his head. Our eyes meet, hold a moment too long, and I suck in a quick breath as heat zings through me—and dammit, it's not the autumn sun that has warmth pooling between my legs.

OMFG.

With a wrench clasped tightly in his right hand he stares at me, like we're in a goddamn Mexican standoff. I swallow hard, and will myself to move, but can't seem to tear my gaze away. Ah, what was that I said about dim-witted moths?

Close the window, Rachel.

While my brain struggles to call the shots, my body has other ideas. Ideas that involve staying exactly where I am and ogling the hottest guy I'd ever seen. Blue eyes, square jaw, a body I could play Plinko on, and low riding, well-worn jeans that accentuate bulges in all the right places, and holy hell, the man has a lot of right places. Want prowls through me, hitting every erogenous spot along the way.

Just shut the window already.

He shifts his stance and taps the wrench against his leg as he looks up am me. A small grin touches his mouth, and that's when I realize I'm half naked. *Please, ground, open up and swallow me.* After hearing the girls, he probably thinks I'm trying to lure him to my room, fix that dry spell I've been going through. I grip the window ledge tighter and slam it down, putting the brakes on my body's reaction, and shutting out six delicious feet of hard muscle and pure testosterone. This is so not what I need right now. Coffee. Yeah, that's what I need. Lots and lots of coffee.

I hurry to the kitchen and shove a pod into the Keurig. I pour milk into a cup and set it on the spill tray. As I wait for the coffee to percolate, I wander into the main level bath-room and glance in the mirror. I look at myself and try to imagine how I appeared through the blue-eyed mechanic's eyes. I see black smudges under tired eyes, boobs that only look big because I'm slender from work, school and lack of proper nutrition and rest. My hair is...wait... I grab a fistful of my curls and examine them closer. Oh, God, pizza sauce.

Could this day get any worse?

Christ, even if he did hear my roommates, I'm sure he'd never look twice at a girl like me—especially the way I look now. A guy like him probably goes out with women who are a little more put together, sexier. Although I have to say in the two months I've lived here, I've never seen a woman come or go from his place. Still, I'm certain a girl next door who always smells like marinara sauce and pepperoni isn't even on his radar.

Good, because I don't want to be.

The coffee machine beeps and I hurry back to the kitchen. I grab the mug to take a big sip. Heavenly. Desperate for a shower, to wash last night's work from my hair, I hurry back upstairs to my room, hot mug of coffee in hand. I check the time and grab my clothes. Giggles come from Sylvie's room across the hall as I dash into the bathroom. I turn the shower to cool, partly because it's just so hot in the house, and partly because I need to calm my overheated body down. I might be off men, especially big, scary ones like my neighbor, but my body and brain aren't working in sync this morning. Clearly my libido didn't get the memo when I left New York.

I stay under the needle-like spray longer than normal, needing an extra minute to clear my head. When the water turns cooler, I jump out, dry off, and pull on a pair of shorts and T-shirt. I towel try my hair, then tie it back into a ponytail. I forgo makeup. Not only will it melt off my face, I'm not trying to impress anyone or draw any kind of attention to myself. Once done, I grab my purse, shove my textbooks into my backpack, and head for the front door, feeling a little more alive after the coffee.

The hot morning air hits like a slap in the face and I groan. It's October for God's sake. It's supposed to be time for pumpkin spiced lattes. This is more like beach weather. Mother nature needs to get her shit together. I glance at my watch, and judging by the time—thanks to an extra-long shower—I need to get my shit together, too. This morning I'll have to take my car to school, or risk being late for class. The walk to campus is long, around forty-five minutes, but I prefer it on days like today. I need to save my gas money for the colder winter months.

Since my driveway runs parallel to my neighbor's, I keep my head down, toss my backpack into the back seat and climb into the driver's side. Thank God the hottie is out of sight and I don't have to go through the embarrassment of facing him.

I roll my window down and shove the key into the ignition. I turn it, only for the engine to make some god-awful sound and stall out. My heart races quicker. Shit. Shit. Shit. Frustrated, I give the steering wheel a thump with my fist. This can't be happening. I need this car. Need to be able to depend on it if I have to run again. I might be an old junker, but it's all I have. I can't afford a new one. Heck, I'm on such a tight budget, I can't even afford to have this one fixed.

I take a deep breath, throw up a silent prayer, and twist the key again, only for it to cough and gasp, like it's dying a slow and painful death.

No. No. No

A tap comes on the roof, and I turn to see my hot—shirtless—neighbor with his arms braced over the door of my car. He leans down, his beautiful face close to mine. "Need a hand?"

"I...uh...it's not working."

Jeez, way to state the obvious.

He grins, and when I see a cute dimple that contrasts sharply with his chiseled face, I nearly swallow my tongue.

"Yeah, I kind of got that, you know, being a mechanic and all." As he gives off a bad-boy vibe that messes with my common sense, he grabs a cloth from his back pocket, and wipes his hands before leaning into the car, his head practically in my lap.

Holy fuck!

It takes everything, and I mean *everything*, in me not to grab the back of his head and shove it between my legs. My sex practically quivers at the visual. The girls were right. I do need to get laid. I bite the inside of my cheek to stifle the moan rising in my throat.

"What...what are you doing?" I finally manage to ask, and will myself not to writhe restlessly, and show him what a needy girl I really am.

He pulls the hood release, and the front end of my car jumps. His head lifts and once again his face is close to mine.

"Popping the hood." He angles his head, and his eyes narrow. "What did you think I was doing?"

Oh, I don't know. Maybe you were taking this opportunity to go down on me.

"Popping the hood," I say quickly, and try not to think of sex. Dirty sex. Take-me-up-against-the-wall kind of sex. Not that I know anything about that. Sadly.

His laugh is rough and deep as he walks around to the front of the car, and I unbuckle quickly. My legs wobble as I climb out of the driver's seat and follow him. He's grinning when I reach him.

"What?" I ask, my voice raspy.

He touches my cracked windshield washer cap, which I happened to repair all by myself. "Duct tape?" he asks, his voice amused.

"Tools of the trade, right," I say and try not to sound as breathless as I feel. A difficult task considering I'm standing next to a half-naked man that I want to run my hands all over. I mean I've seen shirtless guys before, but come on. This guy is like a freaking viking. He leans forward to fiddle with something, and the movement shows off impressive bicep muscles. I break a sweat as his closeness sends shudders of need between my thighs. Honest to God, the man is a work of art, and all I can think of is no-strings sex—something I've never done before. But that's crazy and reckless and so not me. Truthfully, if I knew what was good for me, I'd slam the hood shut and run in the opposite direction.

I'm about to do just that when he says, "Uh, huh."

"Is...is there something wrong?" Is that my voice? Christ, I sound like I'm whacked out on painkillers.

For God's sake, get it together, girl.

He rubs the scruff on his chin, and I step back, needing a measure of distance before I actually reach out and run my hands over all his hard grooves and deep valleys.

"Plenty," he says again and checks something else. I have no clue what he's doing. I only know that he looks as hot as hell doing it. As he leans over my car, my gaze slides to his ass, committing the way his pants cup his cheeks to memory. The guy could be in a jeans commercial, or better yet, a Calvin Klein underwear ad. I'm a girl, but advertising like that would have me one-clicking the buy button.

My heart hammers as he stands again. He turns toward me, but I'm far too slow to react. His eyes are piercing, almost a deeper shade of blue when my gaze jerks to his, and I can't tell whether he's thrilled or pissed to find me checking him out.

I step closer and look over the engine. "So, what is it?" I ask, disgusted with myself. I should not be fantasizing over this man.

He clears his throat. "I think the first thing we need to do is replace the spark plugs," he answers, his voice a little hoarse.

"Yeah, that's what I was thinking," I say, my head bobbing in agreement.

That grin is back when I look at him. "You know something about cars?"

I shrug. "Sure...and duck tape."

He laughs and says, "It's not..." he shakes his head. "Never mind. So, you agree then, that something's not firing right?"

Firing? Oh, things were firing all right, and lighting up my body like a goddamn Fourth of July celebration.

Damn him.

Damn Mother Nature.

Damn dim-witted moths.

2

JAXON

I grab the rag from my back pocket and swipe a bead of moisture from my forehead, as the girl from the upstairs bedroom stands next to me, looking so goddamn hot in her tight AC/DC t-shirt and ripped jean shorts that her car isn't the only thing close to overheating. If I didn't love the band before, I sure as hell would now.

She might have lived next to me for two months, and numerous times I've glimpsed her moving around her bedroom with little to nothing on, but this is the first time I've been so close to her—and it's making it a little fucking hard to breathe.

Talk about fueling all my college girl fantasies.

Not only is she gorgeous, everything about her, from the swell of her cleavage, her barely-there curves, to legs that go on for miles, reminds me it's been a long-ass time since I've had a woman in my bed. It's not that women are on my *do without* list, which is sizable now that I'm the sole caregiver to a five-year-old girl. It's just that after working all day and being a full-time single parent at night, it leaves little time for anything else. That, and I have to be very careful who I let into my daughter's life. No way will I ever let anyone hurt her again.

My sexy neighbor bends over the hood to examine the car again, and my cock twitches—very well aware of how long it's been since it's been touched, too. I try not to chuckle as she tugs on some wires, acting like she knows what she's doing. A moment later, she stands and shifts from one foot to another, her nervous gaze darting from me, to the cars passing by, back to the engine.

"Will it take long?" she asks, as I resist the urge to adjust my thickening cock.

Probably not.

"Uh..." I search for my words, my hard cock interfering with my brain process.

Her eyes fly back to mine. "The car, I mean. Will it take long?" she explains, like I'd misunderstood what she'd meant the first time. I didn't. I just had my mind on other things that likely wouldn't take long, you know, because of the huge hard on I'm sporting at eight in the morning.

I check my watch. "Not long, but I won't be able to get at it for a bit."

She blinks thick lashes over the prettiest brown eyes I've ever seen. "Um...how much will it cost, do you think?"

Her breathy question has me thinking about plunging my hands through her hair and bending her over the hood so I can fulfill all my dirty college-girl fantasies. All I can think about is fucking her until her roommates hear her screams.

"Have you noticed the temperature gauge going high?"

"Yeah, when I was at the stoplight last week, I noticed that."

"Well then, it's not the spark plugs that are going to set you back. It's the radiator. It needs to be replaced."

"Oh...damn." She chews on her bottom lip and crinkles her nose. That's when her scent hits me. Peaches. Why the fuck does she have to smell like sweet peaches? My goddamn favorite fruit. "Maybe we better forget this."

She starts to back away, and I have no idea why, but I'm not ready for this conversation to be over. "Look, I can probably get you a good deal on one, cut your costs in half, and I can do the labor for free."

Jesus, what the fuck am I doing?

"I can't—"

Just then Cassie sticks her head out the upstairs window. "Daddy, I can't find my shoes."

I shade the early morning sun from my eye and my heart misses a beat the way it always does when I see my little girl. "We came in the back door last night, remember?"

"Right."

Cassie disappears and I hear my neighbor mumbling under her breath. Apparently, a broken-down car, one she can't afford to have fixed, is going to make her late for class.

I shove the rag back into my pocket and close the hood. "What time do you need to be there?"

She blinks up at me. "What?"

The lock clicks into place. "School. What time do you have to be there?"

"Thirty minutes."

"I can get you there on time." I nod toward the window my daughter just stuck her head out of. "I'll drop Cassie off, then take you."

She shakes her head fast. "I don't want to put you out like that."

Put me out? Oh, she can put me out anytime, or better yet, put out for me.

I scrub the scruff on my chin. "It's not a problem... uh...shit, I don't even know your name."

"Rachel," she says.

"Jaxon." I hold a hand out for her to shake it, and she

hesitates, going back to shifting her weight from one foot to the other. Cassie does that when she has to go to the bathroom. But I don't think that's Rachel's problem. Tension vibrates from her, and I take in the almost fearful way she's staring at my hand. Why the fuck is she afraid of me? Is it the murder rap her friends were talking about, or is it something else altogether?

I eye her carefully, note the way she continually casts uneasy glances over her shoulder as she shifts. I might be on the straight and narrow now, but over the years I'd be dragged up and kicked around. I'd survived playground bullies, cruel foster parents, and poverty, so yeah, I know a girl on the run when I see one.

"Jaxon Morgan," I say and continue to hold my hand out, and think back to the night she showed up here, with nothing but a rundown car and her belongings in a backpack. No family or friends to help. While I realize trouble is the last thing I need in my life—with the in-laws trying to prove I'm an unfit parent—I can't just turn my back on her. I'm not looking to be anyone's savior, but Christ, it's obvious this girl could use a fucking break.

"I'm not going to hurt you, Rachel." I roll one shoulder as a strange kind of protectiveness grips me. "Just offering a ride and a deal on some car work. We're neighbors after all, right?"

She shoves her hand into mine, and I give it a squeeze. "Right, sorry...I..." She exhales and gives me a smile, like she wants to start over again. "I appreciate it. Thank you."

"Can you give me a minute to get Cassie's lunch packed?"
"Sure."

"Come have a seat inside the shop. Get out of the sun while I get her ready." She snags her purse from her car, locks the doors behind her and follows me into the service bay, aka the bottom half of my house. I grab a piece of paper from behind the counter and gesture toward my cleanest chair. "Have a seat there, and fill in your contact information."

"Oh, okay. What do you need that for?"

"Just in case I run into trouble working on the car and need to run something by you." I give her a wink. "Since you know so much about fixing vehicles."

She smirks as she fishes a pen from her purse, and that's when I realize how much I like her, how easy she is to be around. Not that I know her. I don't. But I love how she shut down her roommates this morning when they were all staring at me. The only one I like watching me is her. Yeah, I caught her checking me out—and not just this morning.

Dammit, don't go there, Jaxon. Cassie needs stability, and you can't bring trouble into your life.

"I'll be right back." I dash up the stair, tug on a T-shirt and hurry into the kitchen. I grab Cassie's empty cereal bowl and drop it into the sink. It teeters on top of the pile of dishes already stacked high. Cassie comes skipping down the hall.

She holds her sneakers up for me to see. "I found them."

I grin at her, and run my hands over her hair. "Good girl. Are you ready?"

"Yeah, but I want twisted pony, Daddy."

Twisted pony, aka top twisted pony braid. I groan inwardly. Even after watching the braiding ninjas on YouTube, my big fingers struggle to get it right. According to Cassie, we usually end up with Nightmare Moon—a reference to the villain on My Little Pony. Sometimes I swear she asks just to torture me.

"How about we just put it up into a ponytail." My mind rushes back to the no-nonsense way Rachel wears her hair. While I like that, I'd love to pull the elastic out and watch those long curls spill over my sheet. I clear my throat. Fuck man, I need to stop fantasizing about my neighbor.

"Please..." she says.

"Okay, hurry, grab the elastic and brush. I have a customer downstairs and I need to give her a drive because her car is broken down."

As Cassie dashes back down the hall, I reach for her lunch box, but it hits the pile of dishes and two plates clatter to the floor and break.

Fuck. I do not have time for this. "Cassie, don't come in here," I yell out.

I crouch down and pick up the big shards of glass and drop them into the garbage can. One cuts my finger. "Shit." I shove it into my mouth.

"Are you okay?" My head jerks up to see a breathless Rachel standing in the doorway. "Sorry, I heard a crash, and thought you might need some help." Her gaze leaves mine and takes in the state of my kitchen. Fuck, the in-laws are threatening to call child protection services. If they showed up now, I'd surely lose Cassie. But I've been so busy at work, and with Cassie starting kindergarten, I'd gotten a little behind on the housework. Then again, it's also possible I got a little lax because they've been away for the last month, vacationing in the Caribbean. Apparently, their absent daughter, and my 'unfit' parenting hasn't prevented them from jet-setting around the world.

"Excuse the mess."

"No, it's okay," she says quickly, her t-shirt shifting over her breasts as she rests a shoulder against the kitchen door-frame and folds her arms. Does she have any idea how sexy she looks standing there? "You should see my bedroom."

"I...uh...I have seen your bedroom," I say. "It's always clean and tidy."

Her eyes go wide and a blush spreads across her cheeks. "You...you've seen my room?"

"It's across from mine, hard not to, right?"

Hard being the key fucking word here. Cause yeah, that shit's happening between my legs again.

"Yeah, true. I can see yours, too. Not that I'm trying to look or anything. It's just that sometimes when I'm up late studying, you have your light on, and your blinds open, and like you said, our windows are directly across from one another." A nervous laugh catches in her throat. "I could toss you a slice of pizza. Sometimes I bring a pie home with me." As she rambles on, I take in the flush on her cheeks. Damn if she isn't sexy when flustered.

"Rachel."

She stops for a moment, takes a deep breath, and lets it out slowly. "Yeah?"

"Can you hand me the broom?" I gesture toward it, and she steps into the kitchen to hand it to me.

"I'm not like my roommates though," she starts up again. "And I want to apolog—"

"Daddy, what happened?" Cassie gasps as she pokes her head into the kitchen, her big blue eyes wide as she takes in the broken dishes. "You're bleeding." She makes a move toward me, but Rachel runs and grabs her before she can walk on the glass.

"I dropped a couple plates, and it's just a little scratch. Stay there, okay, and get your shoes on. I don't want you to get cut. And say hello to our new friend Rachel. She's the client I'm giving a drive to."

Rachel crouches down to Cassie's height, and smiles at her. "Hello, Cassie. I've seen you around but we've never really met before."

"You're Daddy's friend?"

"Yes."

Cassie crinkles her nose. "You're a girl."

"I am."

"Does the mean you're his girlfriend?"

"No, no," Rachel says quickly and explains the difference between girl friend, and girlfriend.

"You're pretty," Cassie says, and I glance up to see her holding her brush and elastics out. "Daddy was going to braid my hair and make me pretty, too."

"You don't need your hair braided to make you pretty, but how about I do it for you, since your dad has to put a bandage on his hand."

Cassie leans into Rachel. "Daddy makes Nightmare Moon."

"Nightmare Moon, what is that?"

"Her name is Princess Luna but when she's evil they call her Nightmare Moon."

"So you're saying your dad makes evil braids?"

"I can hear you," I say, but my heart is in my throat as I see how quickly my child has taken to our neighbor. Cassie has seen her around of course, and they've waved in passing, so truthfully Rachel isn't a stranger to her. None of the college girls next door are.

Rachel giggles with Cassie, and in my heart I know how much my little girl needs a mother, one who isn't an addict and chose a life of drugs and partying over her family. I tried to help her, I really did, but in the end, she ran off with her dealer, without so much as a glance at us in the rearview mirror. I guess we weren't enough for her to get clean. Then again, I was labeled a lowlife and was never enough for anyone to stick around. But I plan to do everything in my power to be enough for Cassie. Outside of her grandparents I'm all she has.

My in-laws were always worried about me taking care of Cassie—considering my past—when they should have been worried about their own daughter. But they didn't know what was really going on behind closed doors, and I didn't want to be the one to shatter their image of their sweet Sarah, a college-educated girl from an upper-class family who veered off track. They blame me for that, but I was slowing down on the partying scene when I met her, and gave it up completely after Cassie was born.

"I think I want a ponytail, like you," Cassie says, bringing my thoughts back.

"Easy enough." Rachel holds her hand out for the brush and elastics, and Cassie hands them to her.

Rachel stands, and turns Cassie around. As she combs out my daughter's hair, I sweep up the rest of the glass, wash and bandage my finger, then grab Cassie's lunch from the fridge. I drop the food into her plastic lunchbox, and look up to find the two girls chatting quietly.

"Are you two whispering about me?" I ask

"No," they both say in unison, but from the grin on Rachel's face, I know it's a lie.

"All right, come on. Let's get you both to school."

"You go to school?" Cassie asks Rachel as we make our way downstairs and back outside.

"I do?"

"What grade are you in?"

"Well, I'm in college?"

"What's college?"

Rachel glances at me and I shake my head. "Chatty Cassie," I say.

I open the door to the back seat as Rachel grabs her backpack from her car. "In you go, kiddo."

Cassie climbs into her car-seat and buckles herself in. "Good?" I ask.

"Good?" she says and picks up her mock iPad and turns it on. As music blares, Rachel slides into the passenger seat. Once we're all buckled up, I back out of the driveway and head to Cassie's school.

Rachel casts me a glance. "You have your hands full."

I scrub my chin and flick on my signal. "Yeah. She's definitely a full-time job, but I wouldn't change it for the world." Rachel shifts restlessly beside me, and I don't miss the curiosity in her big brown eyes. "What?"

"It's not my business, but I take it her mom's not in the picture."

I stiffen and grip the steering wheel tighter, and Rachel holds her hands up, palms out. "Sorry, none of my business. I wasn't trying to pry."

"No, it's okay. I just..." I pause, not wanting to divulge too much about myself. "You're right, her mom's not in the picture. She left a couple years ago and we've not seen her since. It's just Cassie and me."

"I'm sorry, Jaxon."

"Yeah, me too," I say, and clench down on my jaw.

"I was thinking..."

I cast her a quick glance, note the way she's playing with the straps on her purse. "About?"

"That you could use a little help around your place, and with Cassie. Everyone needs a break once in a while right? You're giving me one with my car."

"What are you suggesting?"

"That maybe I could help you around the house. Cook, clean, babysit, teach you how to braid Cassie's hair," she says with a grin. "Although I hear you make a mean Nightmare Moon."

I laugh at that. "Yeah, I guess you're right. What's the going rate for something like that?" I ask. I'm not hurting for money. I have a very successful business, and have been thinking about hiring someone to help me with the house. I just haven't found the time to look more into it. That, and I don't trust too many people with my belongings—time in juvenile hall will do that to you—or with my daughter.

"Well, I was thinking, instead of money, I could spend the

next couple weeks working off the repairs to the car. You're helping me, I'm helping you."

"Tit for tat?"

Shit, now I'm thinking of her tits.

"Yeah, exactly."

I mull that over as I pull up to Cassie's school. I jump out as she unbuckles herself. The second I open her door, she hops from the car and is about to take off until I bend to give her a hug and kiss. "I'll see you later, kiddo."

"Bye, Daddy. Bye, Rachel," she says and I wave to the playground monitor as Cassie runs to catch up to her friends. I slide back into the car and pull in to traffic.

"Okay, so tit for tat. I like it."

I like it a lot. Which is a real fucking problem.

"Um, just one thing you should know, Jaxon."

"What's that?"

She continues to twist the strap of her purse. "What you heard this morning...from my friends."

I shake my head and laugh. "I heard a lot from your friends."

"Yeah, but the part about—"

"Me having killed someone. For the record, I never killed anyone. Gave a few good beatings to a few bad people who deserved them, but I never murdered anyone."

Rachel nods her head. "Good to know, but I'm talking about—"

"You needing to get laid?"

3

RACHEL

Rachel

OMFG.

Jaxon might not have killed anyone, but I sure as hell plan to. The second I get home, there are four necks I'm going to break. Slowly. Painfully. Ecstatically. Okay, yeah, I get it. I was about to bring it up, set the facts straight, but hearing those words coming from his mouth, all sexy and blatant and suggestive like that—it's possible I imagined the suggestive part—well that's shit is messing with my head, and my body.

"I...I..." Jesus what am I supposed to say?

Oh, yes, they were right. I do need to get laid. Are you up for that job, too?

"Hey, it's okay," he says. "I know they were just giving you a hard time."

I swallow. "I don't want you to get the wrong idea about me. I'm just offering to help you out with the house and Cassie. A business arrangement, that's all." Lord knows I'm off men. Not only am I a bad judge of character—guys seem to be one thing only to end up being something else entirely —I'm not about to let anything or anyone derail me again. I want to be a lawyer. I want to champion legal causes for the greater good of society and help those in need of assistance who might not otherwise be able to afford it. I want to help children, and other victims of domestic abuse. The subject is very near and dear to my heart.

Muscles tense, he nods, and stares straight ahead. "I know. That's all I want, too. Strictly business," he says, a guarded note in his voice.

"Okay, good," I say, not wanting to examine the weird, unwanted ball of disappointment settling in my gut. "I can come by tonight and help get the place cleaned up." I glance at my watch. "My shift at Pizza Villa doesn't start until eight, so I have plenty of time."

As he drives, I take in his perfect features, the tattoos on his body. Do they have a deeper meaning? Is Cassie's mother's name on there? Not that it's any of my business. Nor do I want it to be. But he did say he was sorry she was gone.

"Perfect. I'll get your spark plugs fixed and look for a radiator core." He casts me a glance. "So, uh, these roommates of yours. They seem a bit younger, maybe a little less mature than you."

"They are. They're all first year. I'm fourth. Still, I don't think I was ever that juvenile." I never had the luxury.

He shrugs, and spears his finger through his hair, mussing it up and making him look impossibly sexier. "Just girls having fun."

"I don't have time for fun. I never did," I say, then mentally kick myself. He doesn't need to know those things about me.

Stop blabbering around him, already.

"I remember fun," he says and grins. "At least I think I do." I laugh with him. "How did you end up rooming with four freshmen?"

"I transferred here—"

"From New York," he states.

I stiffen in my seat. "How do you know that?"

"Your license plate."

I relax, and look at him closer. For a big, scary tattooed guy, he's pretty observant. "I transferred last minute, because Penn State is where I ultimately want to go to law school." Not a lie. But I'm not about to tell him about my crazy ex. We both clearly have secrets in that arena.

"Law school. I'm impressed."

"A single dad who works all hours and takes good care of his daughter. I'm impressed."

"All hours? How do you know that?"

"Neighbors, remember."

He holds my gaze for a moment, and says, "And yet it took two months and a broken car for us to speak."

"We're both busy. Cassie is a full-time job as it is. You're doing a great job with her, by the way."

A garbled sound catches in his throat. "I'm not sure about that. You saw the house."

"It's just a few dirty dishes, Jaxon." His mouth turns down, and I get the sense there is more going on with him. I should leave it at that but instead find myself asking, "What?"

"It's just... My fucking in-laws are trying to get custody of Cassie, trying to prove I'm an unfit father. Shit, if they showed up and saw the state of my house..." His voice falls off as he rubs his hands over his chin.

My heart pinches. "I'm sorry."

"I can't lose her. She's all I have."

"Then it's a good thing my car broke down, because now you have me." Something moves into his eyes, something that looks like heat as he glances my way. "I mean, now you have me to help out," I clarify.

"Yeah," he says quietly.

He takes the corner and I lean into him. "You can drop

me off there," I say and point to my lecture hall. He pulls the car over and I unbuckle.

"Do you have a drive home?"

"I can walk, or take the bus. It's a nice day."

"I pick Cassie up at two. I can swing by if you need a lift. Just text me."

"I don't have your number."

"I have yours, so I'll send you a text."

I smile at that. Was he really one of the nice guys? I honestly don't know, being a jerk magnet and all, and truthfully, I don't want to know anything more than I already do. This is business only, and I don't care if he's six million degrees hot. I don't want anything more, and clearly he doesn't either. We both have secrets, and at the end of a busy day, neither of us has time for anything else that might complicate our worlds.

"Okay, thanks," I say, with zero intentions of texting. I grab my backpack, and exit the vehicle. As he flicks on his signal, waiting to pull back into traffic, I give him a wave, and turn to find a couple of my classmates walking toward me.

"Who the hell is that hottie?" Allison asks as we all start walking to class.

"My neighbor," I say with a shrug, not wanting them to read anything into it. "My car broke down and he gave me a lift."

"That man can give me a lift anytime, anywhere," Sue says. "Preferably to his bed."

The sudden image of me on his bed rushes through my brain and has heat spreading though me. Ah, what was that I just said about not wanting anything more?

I cast a quick glance over my shoulder, and when I find Jaxon watching me, I jerk back around and pick up my pace. "Let's hurry or we're going to be late."

I spend the rest of the day going from class to class, trying to concentrate on the words my professors are saying when my mind wants to keep straying back to Jaxon—to my phone. Why hasn't he texted yet?

Cut it out, Rachel!

After one meeting, the man is proving to be a distraction I don't need. I should have somehow found the money to pay him instead of offering my services.

Tit for tat.

Oh, God.

Midafternoon rolls around and I grab a muffin, my stomach growling since the only thing I've put in it all day was a cup of coffee. I munch on it, and start toward home, the heat of the day falling over me. Maybe I should have accepted Jaxon's offer and caught a ride with him. Then again, the less time I spend around him the better.

I turn the corner and as I walk along the sidewalk, I spot Cassie and Jaxon. I grin when I see her coveralls—a familiar sight. Poor girl is going to grow up to be a tomboy. What she really needs is female influence in her life. I'd lost my mom in my teens, and that was hard. I can't imagine what it's like for Cassie to have no mother. Jaxon clearly didn't want to talk about it. Did he still love her? Is that why I've not seen him with any other woman in all the time I've been here? He's waiting for the love of his life to come back? If that's the case I really need to stop drooling over him—and even if it's not.

Normally I'd give Cassie a wave and dart inside, but since they're working on my car, I stop. "How's it going?"

Cassie's head pops up from beneath the engine bonnet. "We fixed your spark plugs," she says, a spot of grease on her face. I can't help but grin at her cuteness, the fact that she has the same blue eyes as her father.

"Why thank you, Cassie," I say. Jaxon helps her from the crate she's standing on, and that's when I notice he's still wearing the T-shirt he tugged on this morning.

Too bad.

What, wait! Oh, God.

"Why don't you go in the backyard and play?" He rubs her head and she dashes toward the swing set.

"Is it fixed?" I ask.

He nods, and wipes his hands on a rag. "But I have bad news."

"Really?"

"I went over your entire car and your tie rod end is going. It's not safe to drive until I can get it fixed."

I do a mental calculation of the money in my bank account, and how many more horrible shifts I'll have to take on at Pizza Villa. "How much will that cost?"

"Nothing. You're working it off, remember."

Warm from my walk home, I pull my t-shirt away from my body a couple times, fanning my skin as I think about that. "I know, but that's pushing it. I can't expect you to do all this work for cleaning and babysitting services." Jaxon's gaze drops to my chest as I cool my body, and for a second I get the feeling that he has other ideas on how I can work off my debt. I should be enraged. I really should be. But goddammit, I'm not.

He makes a snorting sound. "I'm getting more out of this trade than you."

"I don't know about that."

"You've seen my place, right?" He averts his eyes to check on Cassie playing, and I can't help but take that opportunity to look him over—again. My gaze drops, takes in the nice fit of his jean, the thickness of his thigh muscles. What was it the girls called him? Slurpalicious. Yeah, that was it, and okay, I'll admit it. I'd like to lick him from head to toe and back up again.

"Do you want to get started?"

"Get started?" I ask.

WTF.

Please tell me I didn't say any of that out loud.

He gestures toward his house. "On the cleaning. You said you'd get at it after school."

"Right, of course."

"What did you think I meant?"

Oh, that I could start licking you from head to toe.

"The cleaning," I say quickly. "Just let me drop my books off inside, and I'll be right back." I hurry to my house and can almost feel his eyes burning into my back. I don't dare look to check, though, but I am questioning my sanity. Do I even know what I'm getting into, inserting myself into this man's life? No. But he's good with his daughter, and I need my car fixed, so I need to do what I need to do.

But will I sleep with him?

What the hell?

I'm not one for one-night stands or quick flings, and sleeping with him has nothing to do with this arrangement. We both made that clear.

Oh, but you want to.

I give my head a good hard shake to get it on straight and step inside the front door, only to hear music blaring from the kitchen. I walk down the hall and find my roommates drinking at the kitchen table. I should have expected it. It's Friday night after all, and another party at our house. Fortunately, I'll miss most of it, thanks to a late-night shift at Pizza Villa. Jeez, who would have ever thought I'd be looking forward to that.

Sylvie jumps up when she sees me and her drink spills over the side of her glass. "We've been waiting for you to get home."

"Why?" I ask, and go to the fridge. I take out the water and pour myself a glass.

"Don't 'why' us," Becca says. "We saw you leaving with the hottie next door."

Val holds her hands up and waves her fingers toward herself. "Come on, spill."

I take a long drink, and set the glass in the sink. "There's nothing to spill. He gave me a ride that's all."

"A mustache ride?" Becca asks. I glare at her, and she frowns.

"So I take it you didn't do the nasty with him?" Sylvie says.

Jesus.

"No, Sylvie. My car broke down, he's fixing it, and gave me a ride so I wouldn't be late for school."

"That's it?" Becca says, clearly disappointed in me.

"Well..." I say, unable to help myself from teasing them a bit. "There is one other thing."

Sylvie squeals. "I knew it. Tell us."

"Since I'm broke, he, and when I say he, I mean Jaxon, agreed that in exchange for fixing my car, I'd—"

"Fuck him!" Sylvie says and starts clapping.

As the four girls go ballistic, I fold my arms until their shrieks die down. When they finally settle, I say, "Sorry to disappoint you all, but all I'm going to do is clean and babysit for him."

Becca grins at me. "Say what you want, Rachel. I can guaran—fucking—tee, that after spending time at his place, you'll end up in his bed. I mean, you're only human, right?"

"Right," Val says. "And I am so freaking jealous, but I'll get over it if you promise to give us all the details."

"Contrary to what you girls believe, there will be no details," I say.

"What's his last name?" Becca asks, grabbing her phone. "Let's creep him on Instagram."

"I don't know his last name," I fib. No way do I want them stalking him online.

"Nameless sex. I love it," Val says.

"I will not be having nameless or any kind sex with him," I say, and keep to myself that I had been thinking just that thing when he was diagnosing my car.

Becca frowns. "How come you're not on social media, Rach?"

"I don't have time for it," I say, a partial truth. After my ex-boyfriend threatened to kill me if I left him, I stripped my identity from the Internet so he couldn't track me down. "Now, if you'll excuse me. I have to go. Jaxon is expecting me."

I turn, and exit the room. As I make my way up the stairs to drop my books off, I can hear their comments.

"Yeah, expecting you to bend over the coffee table for him."

Giggles.

"Or expecting you to get down on your knees and take him deep."

More giggles.

"Better yet, he's expecting you in a hot little French maid outfit obeying his every command. I have one from last Halloween that I didn't end up wearing," Sylvie shouts. "You can borrow it if you want it as long as it gets some action and you give me all the details."

I might be rolling my eyes at my roommates, but there is a part of me that's listening, visualizing all those acts with the hot daddy next door. Heat prowls through me, and I hurry to my room, drop my books on my bed, and step up to my mirror. I give myself a once over, and pinch my cheeks to add a little color.

A noise outside my windows jolts some sense back in to me, and I take in a breath, let it out slowly, and make my way to my neighbor's. I find Jaxon and Cassie inside the shop. The music is on, so I can't hear what he's saying to her, but from the intent look on her face it must be something very important.

My heart pinches. It can't be easy being the mother and father in a relationship. Jaxon looks up and I wave awkwardly. He turns the music down.

"I'm not interrupting anything, am I?" I ask

"Nope," he says. "You can head on up if you want. I'm going to finish some things here, then go over Cassie's homework with her."

"I can do that." When his head rears back, I realize I've overstepped. I'm here to cook and clean, not step in to do mommy things with Cassie. "Oh, sorry, I just meant, I could watch her if you were busy in the shop."

He scrubs his chin and looks around. "Actually it would really be helpful. I need about an hour to finish this job." He points to the car up on hoists, one that wasn't there this morning. "It's a rush job for a buddy. I was going to work on it after Cassie went to bed, but if I could get it done now, that would give me more time to read with her before she goes to sleep."

My chest squeezes. "Sure, I'm here to help with anything, Jaxon. Anything at all. All you have to do is ask."

His head dips, as his eyes lift to move slowly over my face, and my heart nearly stops as the blue bleeds into the black. Jesus, did he take my words to be sexual? And why does everything *feel* so electrical between us. Like we could light up a city block in a black out. For a week.

"Cassie," I say quickly, and hold a hand out to her. "Why don't you come on up with me, and we can set you up at the kitchen table while I tidy."

Cassie looks at her dad, and he explains. "Rachel is going to be our new housekeeper for a little while. She's going to help with the dishes, laundry and even babysit you, and I'm going to fix her car for her."

"Oh, okay," Cassie says, taking it all in stride. "Gina has a babysitter sometimes. She lets her stay up late and eat ice cream."

Jaxon laughs as he helps her from the crate she's standing on. "Nice try, kiddo."

I laugh with Jaxon as his precocious child takes my hand. She chats endlessly about some boy at school named Jacob who pulled her ponytail as we climb the stairs. I shove a full basket of dirty laundry out of our path, and usher her into the kitchen and she hops up on the chair.

"What do you have for homework?" I ask.

"I have to draw a picture of my family."

"Oh that's nice."

She frowns. "Daddy says I can put Mommy in the picture if I want. It's up to me."

I nod. That must have been what they were talking about so intently. I help empty her backpack, and clean out her lunch box.

"Why don't you go ahead and get started and I'll tidy up the kitchen."

She dumps a box of crayons on the table and starts humming as I turn my attention to the dishes. I fill the sink with water, take a cloth to wipe down the counters, then wash and dry all the dishes. As I dry, I take a peek at the drawing.

I grin when I see the picture of her dad. A big stick man, with a circle around his biceps, to represent bulging muscles I assume. Beside her father is a little girl with her hair in a ponytail, and two other people, a man and a woman. "That's very good, Cassie."

"I don't want to put Mommy in the picture."

"Well, you don't have to." My heart hurts for the little girl as I put my hand on her head and run her ponytail through my fingers. "Who are the people beside you?"

"That's Grandma and Grandpa. Grandma always wears pretty beads." She adds in a bunch of circles around the neck.

I gaze at her grandparents. She only drew one set, and I wonder about that. Are they from her mother's or father's side of the family? If the mother's, does Jaxon not have his parents, or any siblings, or is he as alone in this world like I am?

"Do you have any cousins, Cassie?"

"What's a cousin?"

Guess that answers my question.

A noise at the door catches my attention. "How's it going up here?"

The second I look at Jaxon, take in his hard, athletic body and gorgeous blue eyes, my damn ovaries contract. Jesus, no man should walk around looking that good. "Cassie was just telling me about her grandparents, and how her grandma likes to wear beads." Unable to help myself I ask. "The in-laws you mentioned?"

He gives a curt nod, and then says, "Thanks, Rachel." Clearly not wanting to talk about them, he steps past me, and his warm scent reaches my nostrils. "I really appreciate this." He grabs a bottle of water from the fridge and cracks it open, and I watch carefully—too carefully—the way his muscles pull tight as he swallows. He wipes his mouth with the back of his hand and casually says, "I'm making spaghetti for supper. You can stay if you like."

"Thanks, but I have to hit the books before I go to work. I'm going to toss a load of laundry in the washer for you, then take off. I can come back tomorrow and do the floors and whatever else needs to be done. On my nights off, I can even prepare dinner for you both, too. I'm a pretty good cook."

"Then I might take you up on that, because my only specialty is spaghetti and it comes from a jar."

"I like spaghetti, Daddy."

"I know you do, honey."

Grinning, I set the dishtowel down, and make my way to the laundry basket. Once I get the load of laundry going, I peek into the kitchen. "See you both tomorrow."

Jaxon's eyes lift, and when he directs those bedroom blues at me, it's possible to forget every sane thought. "I look forward to it," he says.

I look forward to it.

Oh, God, so do I and I really wish that wasn't the case. I give a finger wave to Cassie and take off like the hounds of hell are chasing me. I hurry home, grab a quick sandwich, study for a bit, then head into work. The pizza shop is just around the corner so it's a quick walk.

Many hours later, after a long night of marinara sauce and pepperoni, I head home, but as I walk toward my place, I can hear the music. I groan. The damn sorority party is in full swing this time of night. Jesus, I wish I could afford my own place.

Head down, I step inside and hurry upstairs. I knock on the bathroom door, desperate for a shower, only to be answered with giggles. Great. I stomp down the hall, go into my room and slam the door shut. I toss my purse on the bed, and flop down beside it.

Just then my phone pings, and I grab it, but when I see who the text is from, I jackknife up, my heart climbing into my throat.

Hey.

Should I answer? Maybe this is the text Jaxon had been meaning to send me all day, to exchange contact information, and he's not looking for a response. I touch my screen, and run my fingers over that one word and a warm shiver I don't want to feel travels through my blood. I slowly climb from my bed, and inch forward to see if he's in his bedroom. When

I catch him standing at his window, staring directly into mine, my nerves fires.

OMFG.

I inch back, and my phone pings again. *You there?*

I run my thumbs over the screen. *Yes, just getting in from work.*

I know.

My pulse jumps. How did he know? Was he waiting up for me? Wait, maybe he needed his bathroom cleaned right away or something. I did tell him anything he needed, right? But seriously what could he possibly need from me at midnight?

Sex.

Shit, don't go there, Rachel.

Saw you coming home. Kind of noisy over there.

Worry zings through me. *Are they keeping you awake?*

No, I'm a night owl, and Cassie's room is on the other side of the house. She's asleep.

I exhale a measure of relief. I don't want him calling the cops and bringing attention to us…to me.

I wish I could say the same. I'm never going to get any sleep.

Come to the window.

Oh, shit.

Still dressed in my ugly brown work uniform with sauce in my hair, I slowly walk to the window. My heart crashes against my ribcage as he comes into view.

I watch him as he texts me. *Open it.*

I slowly slide the pane up, and give a stupid wave. "Hi," I say, feeling far too breathless when I see him standing there in nothing but his jeans.

"Hi," he returns, and leans toward me a bit, his body lighting up beneath the big full moon.

I run my hand through my hair, painfully aware of the state I'm in. "Excuse the mess of me." I give a nervous laugh.

"I...work...Pizza Villa." I roll my eyes. "I seriously need to find another job."

He grins, and my blood rushes. "You look great."

He thinks I look great!

"Yeah, well you're only saying that because you can't really see me in this light, and be thankful you're not in the same room. I smell like pepperoni."

His laugh is low, rough, like a woolen blanket being slid across my nipples. "I like pepperoni."

"Maybe I should bottle it, use it for perfume."

What the hell am I saying?

"Guys would go crazy." He laughs. "We could call it Meat."

"I think we're on to something."

He gestures with a nod behind him. "You want to come over until the noise dies down?"

"Oh, did you need me to clean for you? Pack Cassie's lunch?"

"No, tomorrow is Saturday. She doesn't have school. I thought, well, since I can't sleep and you're not going to get any sleep with that noise, that maybe we could watch a movie or something."

Or something...

"I...uh...been waiting to get a shower. I wanted to get out of these clothes right away, but the door is locked and when I knocked all I heard were giggles. I don't even want to know what's going on in there."

He soft chuckles curls through me and settles deep between my legs. "Sex in the bathroom at a sorority party. I wouldn't expect anything less."

As soon as the word 'expect' leaves his mouth, every dirty little thing my roommates said earlier comes rushing back in a whoosh.

"... expecting you to bend over the coffee table for him."

"...expecting you to get down on your knees and take him deep."

I swallow. Hard.

"You can shower over here, if you want. I even have clean towels, thanks to you."

I visualize myself in his shower, and picture the curtain sliding open and Jaxon joining me, soaping my body with those big hands and then carrying me to his bed, where he does the most delicious things to the needy juncture between my legs.

Yes, please...

But I shouldn't get involved with my neighbor. I'm trying to keep a low profile, and he's the kind of man that draws lots of attention. And not only do I have school to concentrate on —he's a sexy distraction I don't need—I don't know him. He could end up turning out to be crazy like my ex. I'm just getting settled in here, and would hate to have to find another place to live if he turns into a crazy stalker because we got intimate.

Then another thought hits. Maybe, I'm making too much of this. Maybe he's just being friendly, and doesn't have sex on the brain like I do. But what if he does...

Say no, Rachel.

Say no, and go to bed with sauce in your hair.

"So what do you say?" he asks.

"Yes."

Dammit.

4

JAXON

Jaxon

W hat the fuck am I doing?

Inviting my sexy neighbor over to my house is one thing, but offering up the use of my shower, well, that's something else entirely—something stupid. Why the fuck am I pushing to spend more time with her? What we have is a business arrangement, and Cassie doesn't need someone in her life who might up and run at a moment's notice. Besides that, how the hell am I going to keep my dick soft, and my hands to myself knowing she's in there naked, running *my* soap all over her lush body? I might not have had a woman beneath me in a long time, but the truth is, until now, none had ever made me so painfully aware of my abstinence.

What the fuck is it about the sorority girl next door that's gotten under my skin, invaded my thoughts? I'm a father, for Christ's sake—at least seven years her senior—trying to raise a child alone. I'm overprotective of my little girl. A dutiful dad who is careful who he brings into her life.

But you're still a man.

The soft knock on my front door drags my thoughts back.

I pad quietly across the room and try to pull off casual when I open it, but seeing Rachel standing there on the stoop, her clothes stained from work, her cheeks a sexy shade of pink, and some kind of red sauce in her hair, it's all I can do not to drag her to me, and kiss those full lips until she's gasping for breath. I suck in air, expecting the smell of pepperoni to tame my cock, but what I get instead is peaches. Goddammit, she still smells like sweet peaches, and it's fucking with me, hard.

"Hi," she says, her voice low, as she gives me another one of those awkward, nervous waves that kind of turns me on.

Yeah, I know. There's something seriously fucking wrong with me.

I open the door and wave her in. "Want a drink first, or do you want to get out of those clothes right away?"

"What?" she asks her eyes wide as her hand tightens on the edge of the doorframe.

"You said you wanted out of your clothes right away, so I was wondering if you wanted a drink or did you want to get right into the shower." I take in the tension in her body as she lets go of the doorframe and straightens.

She nods fast, and her ponytail bounces. "Right."

"What did you think I meant?"

"Shower," she says quickly. "You wanted to know if I wanted to shower right away." As she rambles, I'm not so sure that's what she thought at all. From the way her chest is heaving, to the heat in her eyes—not to mention the tension arcing between us—I'm beginning to believe she wants me as much as I want her.

So, what am I going to do about that?

Nothing.

Zilch.

Zero.

We both agreed this was a business deal, and there are many reasons I have to leave it at that.

"So what is it?" I ask, and rake my hand through my hair.

Her gaze follows the movement, then drops to my chest. "Rachel?" I ask.

She tears her gaze away. "I think I'd like to get cleaned up."

"Sure. Follow me."

She stays close as I lead her down the hall. I lower my voice. "That's Cassie's room, the spare room is beside her." I jerk my finger to the right. "I'm over here, and right at the end you'll find the bathroom." I step to the side so she can go by me. "You'll find towels in the cabinet."

"Thanks, Jaxon," she says quietly. "I really appreciate this."

"Not a problem."

I stand there until the bathroom door closes. I hear her fumble around for a moment, then I realize what she's doing.

"There's no lock," I say. "I took it off years ago when Cassie accidently locked herself inside.

"Oh, okay.'"

I listen for a moment, hear the rustle of clothing, then exhale painfully as I try not to picture her getting undressed, climbing into my shower—the same shower I jerked off in after I dropped her off at school.

Motherfucker.

Despite the heat inside my place, I go to my room and tug on a t-shirt, then plop down onto the sofa. My mind is racing as I flick through the stations, unable to keep my focus on anything other than Rachel naked in my shower. I reach down and adjust my cock in my jeans, and listen to the water run.

Ten minutes pass, and I'm so damn restless I jump up and go to my tidy kitchen. I stare into the fridge, memorize the contents, then grab a beer. Shit, I wish I had wine on hand to offer her. There hasn't been a bottle in the fridge in years, not since my ex took off. I make a mental note to find out what

Rachel likes and pick some up. As I take a pull from the bottle, I walk down the hall, listen outside the bathroom door for a second.

I'm about to turn when I hear a loud shriek. Shit.

"Jaxon," she cries out and I reach for the doorknob, but stop myself before opening it. "Oh, my God," she yells. "The cold water tap broke off, and I can't get it turned off."

Fuck, I meant to tell her it was loose.

"I'm coming in," I say. I open the door and avert my eyes. I grab a towel and hold it up. "Here, climb out. I'm not looking."

She jumps from the shower and her teeth are chattering as she wraps herself in the towel. I step around her, grab the broken handle and screw it back on, getting soaked in the process. After a few good twists, I manage to get the water turned off. Christ, this place is falling apart around me. Between Cassie and work, I've had little time to get everything fixed. Maybe I needed help more than I realized.

"I need to get this replaced." I turn back to her, and her eyes are wide as she stands there staring at me, her body shivering. "I'm sorry, Rachel. I never even thought to tell you."

Yeah, because all I could think about was her naked.

"It's okay...." she says and shivers some more.

"Come here." Without thinking I pull her into my arms, and run my hands up and down her back to create heat with friction. Only problem is, I'm suddenly aware that I have a naked Rachel pressed against me, and she's quivering all right, but now I'm not so sure it's because she's chilled. "Better?" I ask and step back.

"Yes, thanks. And the shower was great until I tried to turn the tap off. I used your soap. I hope you don't mind." She brings her arm to her nose. "I smell like you now. I mean not that I know what you smell like. Oh, and you're not going to believe this." She gives a nervous laugh and rolls her eyes.

"I didn't even bring any clean clothes with me. I think all that music and the partying distracted me."

Walk away dude.

"It's okay, you can borrow something of mine."

Don't go down that road, Jaxon. Seeing her in your clothes will be a total mind fuck.

"Oh, are you sure you don't mind?" she asks and pushes a wet strand of hair from her face.

"No," I say and take a small step toward her, until our bodies are almost touching again. Her breathing changes, becomes faster. "They'll be a little big on you."

She gives a breathy laugh. "I can't believe I forgot clean clothes."

"I probably would have forgotten too. Been a bit distracted myself."

"The music?"

"No."

"What then?"

I take a deep breath and let it out slowly. Once I start down this road, there will be no turning back, but fuck, I can't seem to help myself around her. "You," I say, and run a wet strand of hair between my fingers. "I'm distracted by you, Rachel."

"Oh," she says breathlessly, her towel slipping a bit. She grabs it, holds the knot in her hand, and I cup her cheek.

"When I saw you come home, moving around inside your bedroom, all I could think about was tasting you, feeling you beneath me." I give her a nudge and she starts walking backward as I guide her out of the bathroom and into my room. "I spend way too much time at that window waiting to get a glimpse."

"Oh," she says again, and wets her bottom lip likes she preparing it for my mouth.

Bodies in sync, like we've been doing this dance for years, she matches my steps, until we're in my bedroom.

"To be honest, I've been distracted by you for a long time. I've wanted you since you first moved in and I saw you moving around your room."

She glances around, her gaze lingering on my window—the one that looks directly into her room—then she looks at my bed.

"Since we're being honest, I...uh...don't think it was just the music that distracted me, Jaxon."

"No?"

"No, I think it had more to do with you coming to your window shirtless. You can't keep walking around like that. It's turning my roommates into dim-witted moths."

I chuckle, and give a little tug on her wet hair until her mouth is open. I put my lips close to her ear, breathe her in. "And you, Rachel. What's it doing to you?"

"Dim-witted moth," she says, and when I laugh against her ear, she quivers against me.

"So, this distraction. What do you think we should do about it?" I ask.

"Well, I think there is only one thing we can do. Otherwise we're going to be doing stupid things, like forgetting our clothes."

"Or hanging out at our window all day."

"Exactly."

"So one thing, huh?" I nudge her, until her knees hit the edge of my bed. "Like sleep together?"

"Yeah, like a no-strings, one-night affair to help get our heads on straight."

"That's very logical thinking."

"I am going to be a lawyer, you know." She taps her head. "Logic is a necessary skill."

Jesus Christ, there is nothing logical in what we were

doing, and we both damn well know it. But that isn't stopping either of us, obviously. And honest to fuck, if she wants me to stop, I will, but it's going to have to be soon, before we go too far down this road.

"As a mechanic, I'm a problem solver, too." I hold my hands up to show her. "But I'm a tactile kind of guy, and have more skill with my hands."

"Oh, God," she squeaks out as her gaze goes to my hands.

"I want to fuck you, Rachel." She gasps at my blunt words, but the fire in her eyes tells me she likes it. "If you don't want that, you need to stop me right now."

"I...I want that, Jaxon."

I walk to my window, close the curtains, then reach for my belt as I go back to her. "Tell me exactly what you want."

"I want tonight. I want you to fuck me."

Fuck, yes.

I remove her hands from the knot on her towel, and she gives a little gasp when the cotton slides down her body. I step back, my heart crashing as I take my time to look at her, too much time apparently, because she starts to fold her hands over her chest.

"Don't," I say, my gaze going back to her face as my cock presses against my zipper. "You're beautiful. So goddamn beautiful, Rachel."

She takes a deep breath, and when her eyes drop, I reach over my shoulders and tug my shirt off. Her eyes dim with desire, and I'm man enough to admit I like the way she looks at me.

"So are you," she whispers and puts one hand on my chest. Her skin is so soft against my body, her touch light as she explores me and it's all I can do not to lose my shit.

I remove her hand, and put both of them around her back and hold them there as I step into her. I dip my head and her breath is warm on my face as she looks up at me.

"This mouth," I say, and close my lips over hers. Her sweet taste explodes on my tongue and a growl I have little control over climbs out of my throat. She moans, sags against me, and her needy sound curls through my blood and arouses me even more.

I angle my head and deepen the kiss, tasting the depths of her and loving the way her body has come alive for me. Our tongues tangle and play as we explore. I free her hands, place mine on the small of her back and tug her against me. I kiss her long, hard and deep, then tear my mouth away needing it on other parts of her body. She rakes her nails through my hair as I bend and bury my mouth in the hollow of her neck, tasting her skin, as I lick and kiss and revel in her scent. Her pulse jackhammers against my tongue and it's a real struggle for me not to bend her over and take her hard. While I'd like to do just that, I don't want to rush tonight.

"Jaxon," she murmurs as I dip lower and pull one taut nipple into my mouth as my hand leaves her back to play with her other breast. I massage gently, rub my thumb over her pert bud, let her sexy noises push me to the edge. "Yessss...."

I suck her nipple in deeper, center it between my teeth, testing her likes and dislikes as I lightly clamp down on it, a vicious little bite. Her breathing becomes faster and she sags slightly. I let go, and lave her softly to ease the sting. I treat her other nipple to my mouth, and she whimpers and writhes against me. The sound drives me on. I glance up at her, take in her closed eyes, the need on her pretty, flushed face.

Fuck, I need to be inside her. But it's too soon. There are other things I need to do to her first, like get my mouth between her legs, my tongue high inside her until she's begging me to make her come.

Needing to savor her, because this is just a one-night thing, I hold her hips and give a gentle shove until she's sitting on my mattress. Her eyes are wide as she glances up at me, and I swallow. I've never seen a sweeter sight. My cock thickens, and she reaches out and places her hand over the aching bulge.

"Jesus, fuck," I say under my breath as she massages my dick.

I drop to my knees, my breath uneven and labored as I grip her thighs and widen them. She leans back, braces her hands behind her, a desperate kind of need in her eyes as she opens herself to me. I gaze at her gorgeous, wet pussy, and when she moves her hips, I wonder what the fuck I ever did to deserve her in my bed.

"Tonight, you're all mine," I say. "I'm going to devour you, Rachel. Own you completely." Her chest rises and falls as she breathes faster, and her heat reaches out to me, sears my blood and hugs my cock.

"Jaxon," she cries out, and inches her legs open more, the passion between us so goddamn explosive it's a bit fucking scary.

I slowly slide my hands up her thighs and press my thumbs to her soaking lips to ease them open. The second I'm greeted with hot pinkness, I let loose a growl, and press my mouth to her sex, eat at her like a man starved. I suppose I am. Considering how long it's been since I've been with a woman. But this sweet, girl next door isn't just any woman. There is something about her that has me forgetting to be careful.

My tongue penetrates, laps at her liquid desire, hot devouring strokes that are carnal in their need. She bucks against me and a strangled moan escapes her as I push my finger into her tightness. She clenches around my finger, her pussy so fucking tight, I'm guessing it's been as long for her as it's been for me.

I groan and circle her clit with my tongue as her taste explodes in my hungry mouth. *Need.* She clutches at me and I unzip my pants, desperate to free my aching cock. The hiss of my zipper fills the room, and Rachel makes a little whimpering sound that curls around me. I soften my tongue, flatten it over her swollen clit, and reach for the hot bundle of nerves inside her.

"Jaxon," she cries out.

"Yeah, you like that?" I ask from deep between her legs.

"Yesss..." she hisses. I grip my cock, run my hand over it as I fuck her with my finger and tongue. I increase the pressure on her clit, and crook my finger inside her body. She sits up straighter, grips my shoulders and meets my glance.

"I...oh..." she says, but it turns to a moan as she comes all over my hand and mouth. My sweet reward. I lap at her, drink in her heat, and when she finally stops spasming, I ease out from between her legs.

My heart is pounding in my ears as I slowly stand, and her eyes go impossibly wider when she sees my pants split open and my hand on my dick.

She wets her mouth and I nearly shoot off then and there. If I put my cock in that mouth of hers there's a good fucking chance I'll release down her throat. But when she licks her lips like that, heat and eagerness in her eyes, how can I not want just that? No goddamn way are we going any farther until she wraps those full lips around me—no matter how torturous.

"Open your mouth," I demand in a soft voice and she instantly obliges. I cup her chin, and push my thumb into her mouth. "You want my cock in here?" I ask, knowing full well from the heat in her eyes that she does. She nods, sucks on my thumb, and I rub my dick harder.

She reaches out to touch me and I remove my hand to give her full access. My balls tighten with that first sweet touch of her fingers. She runs them along the long length of me, touching, exploring, and weighing me in her palm. Fuck man, I'm not sure how much more I can take of that.

She grips my cock a little tighter, and leans in, wrapping her hot mouth around my crown, drinking in the pre-cum. I jerk my hips forward, and try not to destroy her pretty mouth as I hit the back of her throat. She gives a little moan of approval and I fist her hair, the chemistry between us off the charts. Honest to fuck, the last time I felt chemistry like this was...never.

I do my best to hold my control as she works her mouth and hand in tandem. I'll be damned if I come in her mouth. I need my cock inside her. One soft hand cups my balls, gives a gently rub and they tighten, and my fucking release gets ready to make a run for the finish line.

"Stop," I growl, and pull her off my cock. Her mouth is wet, glistening in the light, and I brush my thumb over the wetness. "Get on that bed, and spread your legs for me."

She whimpers and her ass is aimed my way as she darts to the middle of the mattress. She shouldn't have done that. I take her in. Right now, I want in her pussy, tomorrow I'll claim that sexy ass.

Wait, what? There isn't going to be a tomorrow.

But tonight...oh yeah, there is going to be a tonight.

"I'm going to fuck you so thoroughly tonight, make you shatter so hard for me, you're still going to feel me a week from now."

Heat moves into her cheeks, the hot pink color matching her beautiful pussy. "Ohmigod, Jaxon," she says on a breathless whisper.

"Only problem is, I want you so fucking bad, I might just ruin you." I climb onto the bed, position myself between her legs, and run my thumb over her swollen clit, a slow caress that has her writhing beneath me. "But you want that, don't you?"

"I've never been..." she whispers. "Yes, I want to be fucked like that."

I lean forward, grab a condom from the nightstand and quickly roll it on. I angle my head, take in her deep, labored breaths. I pitch my voice low, a strange new tenderness taking up residency inside me. "You've never been fucked like that, Rach?"

Her hair splays across my sheet as she shakes her head. "No. Never."

I'm suddenly spitting mad that no man had ever fucked her properly. But on the other hand, I'm fucking ecstatic. I want to be the guy who gives her exactly what she needs— over and over again. I grip her legs and tug. She locks her ankles at my back and I press my crown to her hot center. "But you want to be fucked like that?" I ask.

"Only by you, Jaxon," she murmurs.

My heart misses one beat, then two when I realize the trust she has in me. "Jesus, fuck," I growl, needing desperately to do right by her. She has secrets, is on the run, and has never been properly taken care of in the bedroom. That shit tugs at something inside me as I jerk forward, and in one long thrust, seat myself high inside her. Her sex tightens around me, spasms and flutters against my cock as I fill her.

Breathe, Jaxon.

I grip her hair and fist it, willing my climax away as need drags me under, until I'm drowning in it. "You feel so good." Lost in lust, and teetering on the edge, I inch out, a slow easy slide that rocks my world. Rachel gasps, and scratches at my back as I glide back in again, the friction doing mind-fucking things to both of us. Her nails rake my skin, but I fucking love it. I power forward, surge deeper, and she moves with me, her hips rising with each hard thrust, welcoming me deeper into her body, yet for some fucking reason I can't seem to get in deep enough. I go at her like a man possessed as our bodies merge, seek the ultimate pleasure of release.

I find her mouth again, tangle my tongue with hers as we fuck. She grows slicker with my deep penetration, and I break the kiss, desperate to see the look on her face as I bring her to climax. Her hands cup my face, and her mouth opens and closes, her lids fluttering rapidly.

"You like me fucking you like this?" I ask.

"Yes."

"You feel so good, Rach."

Too good.

"More...harder," she cries out, and seeing this guarded girl so open and free, her body in my hands as I fuck her hard, does the weirdest things to me.

I inch almost all the way out, and she lifts for me as I slide back inside, her warmth and wetness stealing my ability to think...to breathe.

I slip a hand between our bodies, apply pressure to her clit, and revel in the way she cries out my name as I slam back into her.

"Yeah, that's it, come hard for me."

She swallows, a dry raspy sound that strokes my hard on. I take in the ecstasy on her face as her muscles clench around me, teasing my climax and frying my brain cells.

Restraint a thing of the past, I throw my head back. "I'm there," I say, as I drive impossibly deeper. Seated high inside her, I let go, and concentrate on the points of pleasure. My cock pulses, and the room fades from existence as a supernova climax tears through me. I try to breathe, fill my lungs, but can't seem to remember how. What the ever-loving fuck is going on with me.

"Yesss....." she hisses. "That feels so good."

I collapse on top her, bury my face in her neck as her body softens beneath me. We lay there in the quiet for a long time, and when my post-orgasm bliss finally fades, and reality moves in to take its place, I inch back to see Rachel. I've not had a girl over since my ex left, and if I knew what was good for me, I'd usher her out of my bed before my daughter wakes up. But as I look at my sweet neighbor, take in her spent, sated look, the small smile on her mouth, all I want to do is take her again.

5

RACHEL

A loud bang followed by someone coughing outside my window pulls me awake. I groan, and roll over, searching for the spare pillow to pull over my head, only to find a warm, hard body instead. What the hell? My lids fling open and as I take in Jaxon's nakedness, the sheets at the bottom of the bed, all the dirty delicious things we did last night come racing back in a whoosh.

OMG.

I glance at my own body, find it completely naked, thoroughly fucked. I take in the finger bruises on my hips, remember the hot way Jaxon touched me. As my body stirs again, wanting more, I cover my mouth to stifle the sound crawling out of my throat. Oh, this is not good. Not good at all. I should not have slept with my neighbor, or woken up in his bed. What we have is a business arrangement, but now this changes everything—and not in a good way.

I search the floor for my clothes, only to find Jaxon's. Dammit, my dirty work clothes are still on his bathroom floor. Left with no choice but to slip back into his, I slide from the bed, quieter than as a church mouse at a Sunday sermon. No way do I want him to wake up and be forced to make awkward morning-after conversation. I need to get home, and I need to do it now. Then I need to come up with a new game plan. One where I pay cash for my vehicle repairs so I don't have to spend any more time with this man. Becca was right. No way can I be around him without wanting to do the horizontal mambo. I am, after all, only human.

I tug on his sweatpants, tie them tight at the waist, and reach for his T-shirt. As I slide into it, another bang from outside the window reaches my ears. I tiptoe across the room, and glance outside to see some guy throwing up in our bushes. Great. Just great. I need to find another place to live. I shake my head, and peer through the window into my bedroom. We really do have direct line of sight with one another. Maybe I should get one of the girls to switch rooms with me. When it comes to my hot neighbor, the less temptation the better.

I quietly open the bedroom door, prepared to head home in my neighbor's clothes, and do the walk of shame, but go still when the hinges squeaks. Dammit. A quick look over my shoulder confirms Jaxon is still asleep, and I let go the breath I'm holding. I tug the door quicker, and slip from the room. I hurry to the bathroom, grab my dirty clothes off the floor and dart down the long hall, but my footsteps come to a resounding halt when a little voice sounds behind me.

"Rachel?" Cassie asks. "What are you doing?"

I turn to find a sleepy Cassie rubbing her eye, a teddy bear tucked under her arm. "Good morning Cassie."

She frowns. "I thought you were Daddy."

"Your daddy is still sleeping."

"Why are you wearing daddy's clothes?"

"Ah..."

"Are you doing the laundry?"

I glance at the soiled uniform in my hand. "Ah, well, something like that."

"Sometimes when I sleep over at Gina's house I wear her clothes. I have my own clothes at Grandma and Grandpa's when I sleep over there, but they're in the Carbean right now."

"Carbean?" I ask.

"It's warm there." She widens her arms. "They have a huge pool, bigger than my school."

Ah, Caribbean. They must stay at a resort.

Cassie rubs her belly. "I'm hungry."

Shit. I really wanted to be gone, out of here before Jaxon woke up. Hook ups aren't my thing but how can I possibly walk out on Cassie? I could always wake Jaxon up, but the idea of that sits in the bottom of my stomach like cold oatmeal.

"How about I make you something to eat," I say, wanting to bolt, but unable to turn my back on the little girl when her father is still in bed—a bed where he did such delicious things to me. My body quivers at the memories.

"Are you sick?" Cassie asks.

I take her hand and lead her into the kitchen. "What, no. Why do you ask that?"

She climbs into her chair, her little feet dangling below her. "Daddy says my face gets red when I have a fever. Do you have a fever?"

Oh, she doesn't know the half of it.

"No, it's just been warm lately," I fib. "We're having a heat wave, remember?"

Cassie wiggles her toes. "Daddy says if the heat wave continues, he'll get my pool out for me."

"That sounds like fun."

"You could swim with me."

"I could." Or not. "Now, what would you like for

breakfast?"

"Pancakes."

"Okay." I open the cupboards, and search for a pancake mix. I'm a pretty good cook, but I'm in a hurry this morning, so I go straight for the box. I move a few cans, and a couple of boxes of crackers around. "I don't see any mix," I say.

"What's a mix?"

I make a little square with my hands. "Like a box that the pancake batter comes in."

She shakes her head and her curls bob around her shoulder. "Daddy doesn't use a mix."

"Oh, really?" I ask, a little surprised by that. "What does he use?"

"How about I show you?"

The sound of Jaxon's voice sends little threads of need along my spine. I glance up to find him in a pair of jeans and nothing else, leaning against the doorway, that sexy dimple of his prominent as he grins at me.

"Daddy," Cassie says and holds her arms out. My heart squeezes as Jaxon gives his daughter a good morning kiss on the top of her head, then musses up her hair with his hand.

"Why are you up so early, kiddo? It's Saturday." he asks.

"I heard footsteps," Cassie explains.

I crinkle my nose. "Sorry, I tried to be quiet."

Jaxon comes up beside me as Cassie turns her attention to her teddy bear. "Why didn't you wake me?" he asks quietly.

"You were sleeping so soundly."

"So you weren't trying to sneak out?"

Busted.

"No," I fib. "I thought you could use your rest after..." My words fall off. Jeez, what am I supposed to say? I thought you could use your rest after you fucked me so thoroughly, just like you promised. And yeah, I am going to feel him for all of next week.

His hand brushes mine, a light caress that sends shivers skittering though me. "You didn't have to rush off."

"School. Studying. Busy."

"Yeah?" He inches back, his blue eyes latched on mine, studying me carefully.

"Yeah."

"Rachel," he begins, but stiffens when a knock comes on his door.

Cassie wiggles from her chair, and darts down the hall. "Who could be at your door this early?" Then another thought hits. "I hope it's not the guy from the bushes."

"What guy from the bushes?"

I'm about to explain when voices reach my ear. Jaxon stiffens. "Shit."

I touch his arm, and his muscles are so taut, I'm sure they're about to snap. "Who is it?" I ask quietly.

"The in-laws."

I suck in a panicked breath. "I really shouldn't be here." I'm about to run from the kitchen, sneak out the back entrance, when Cassie comes rushing in with her grandparents behind her.

"Daddy, Grandma and Grandpa are here."

The elderly couple breeze around the corner but come to an abrupt halt when they find me standing there next to Jaxon—dressed in his clothes.

"Oh, and who is this?" the woman with the blue eyes and silver hair asks as she touches her pearls—not beads. Very expensive pearls by the looks of things.

Jaxon opens his mouth but Cassie beats him to it.

"Rachel is Daddy's girlfriend. She does laundry and dishes and is going to babysit me," she blurts out and hops back into her chair. "We're making pancakes, but Rachel can't find the mix. Daddy is going to show her to make them."

The strong scent of expensive perfume wafts before my

nose as Cassie's grandmother smooths her silver hair from her face, the gold bangles on her wrists clanging with the movement.

I fidget uncomfortably, and wait for Jaxon to explain, even though I'm not sure how he can possible explain this without them thinking he's an unfit father who brings random women into his house for sex. Really though, when it comes down to it, that's exactly what I am. We'd only exchanged our first words yesterday, and last night confirmed it was a one-shot deal. None of this was going to help him look like the doting father he really is...unless.

"That's right. I'm Rachel, Jaxon's girlfriend." Jaxon stiffens beside me as I hold my hand out. "Nice to meet you both. I've heard so much about you. Just yesterday, Cassie had to do a family picture for school, and you were both very prominent figures."

"Is that right?" Cassie grandmother says, a smile on her face as she bends to give Cassie a kiss.

Cassie's grandfather—tanned and trim in his dress pants and crisp white shirt—steps forward to take my hand, his bushy brows are drawn tight as his gaze takes me in, carefully, suspiciously. "And here we've heard nothing about you." He casts a quick disapproving glance Jaxon's way.

"That's because you've been away for the last few months, Karl," Jaxon explains.

"The relationship is new, then?" Karl asks as Cassie's grandmother eyes the clean kitchen, her head nodding slowly.

"I've known Jaxon for a few months now," I say. Not a lie. I've 'seen' him and his daughter for a few months, we just hadn't spoken until yesterday.

"What do you do, dear?" Grandmother asks.

"Judy..." Jaxon says between clenched teeth, his tone holding all kinds of warning, but I put my hand on his arm to let him know it's okay.

"I'm a fourth-year student at Penn State. I plan to go into family law next year."

"Oh," she says, her eyes wide from surprise. "Isn't that lovely." But the words are dry on her tongue. She's either unimpressed or doesn't believe me. Her gaze goes to her granddaughter again. "Jaxon always did like the smart ones." Jaxon stirs beside me, a sound catching in his throat, and I touch his arm when I see the real pain in Judy's eyes. She runs her hands over her granddaughter's hair. "I suppose Cassie could use a positive female influence in her life." She arches a brow, and aims a direct look at Jaxon. "And a clean living space."

Ignoring the jibe, Jaxon asks, "What brings you both here so early?"

Judy blinks, and shakes her head like she's pushing haunting memories to the back of her mind. "We just got in this morning, and thought we'd take Cassie for the long week-end. We've missed her."

"Yay," Cassie says and starts clapping her hands.

Jaxon pushes off the counter. "I was going to get out her pool today. It's been so warm here."

"Daddy, pleasssseeee..."

"She can swim in our pool," Karl says, smugness in his voice. "Our below-ground is much better than that rubber thing you blow up and try to squeeze into."

"Daddy..."

Jaxon's chest rises and falls as he takes in air, and while I don't know him well, my guess is he's trying to keep his temper under check. "Let me feed her first," Jaxon says, giving into his daughter's pleas, and Cassie starts clapping again. "We were about to make pancakes."

"No need." Karl holds his hand up, palm out. "She'll have breakfast with us."

Jaxon lifts his daughter from her seat and she says, "Can we have chocolate chips in our pancakes?"

"Of course," Judy says.

"Let's get you packed up, kiddo."

Jaxon disappears down the hall, leaving me with his in-laws. A heavy silence comes over the room, and I glance around, looking for something productive to do as they stare at me. Noting awkward about this at all. I point to the coffee maker. "I'm was just about to make some. Would either of you like a cup?"

They both shake their heads, and I search for something else to say. I'm about to ask them about their tans, when Judy says, "Cassie is a very special girl."

"Yes she is," I agree. "Very smart, too."

"She needs stability."

I think about my own childhood. "All kids do."

"I'm glad you understand that," Karl says, his eyes narrowing. "She can't have people coming and going from her life. It's not healthy."

Dammit, he's right, and I never should have inserted myself into their lives or blurted out that I was Jaxon's girlfriend. I have no idea what happened to Cassie's mother, or why these two seem to hate Jaxon so much, but when Cassie told them I was his girlfriend, I jumped on it. Not because I wanted that to be true. I don't. But because I didn't want them to think he was an irresponsible man who had women coming and going from Cassie's life.

Needing to busy myself, I fill a carafe with water and pour it into the coffee maker. As I reach for the coffee grounds, I shake my head at this insane turn of events, considering less than an hour ago, I was trying to sneak away, prepared never to set eyes on Jaxon again and find another way to pay off my vehicle repairs. Now I'm pretending to be his girlfriend.

Way to make a mess of things, Rachel.

"Do you live here?" Judy asks. The question takes me by surprise. Then again, I am in his clothes so why wouldn't they jump to that conclusion.

"I actually live next door. My bathroom was occupied after work, so I used Jaxon's shower, and forgot to bring a spare change of clothes."

I suck in a breath of relief when I hear footsteps running down the hall, putting an end to the interrogation.

"I'm ready," Cassie says, and leaps into her grandfather's arms. Jaxon tugs on a t-shirt as he comes in behind her,

Cassie reaches out for her grandmother's hand, and I stay put in the kitchen, as Jaxon walks them to the door. I press start on the coffee maker and even though I don't want to eavesdrop, I can't help but hear the tense exchange regarding Cassie's return time on Monday. A few seconds later, I turn to face Jaxon in the kitchen. I expect anger—after all I never should have announced that I was his girlfriend—but what I see instead tugs at my heart.

"Thanks," he says quietly, and drives his hands into his pockets, forcing them lower on his hips.

"You shouldn't be thanking me." I lean against the counter, and fold my arms over my chest. "I think I might have made things worse for you."

"How so?"

"They think I'm your girlfriend, Jaxon."

"Yeah." He frowns. "Why did you do that, anyway?"

"I didn't like the way they were looking at you. Like you weren't a good father. I didn't want then to think you brought a different girl home all the time."

He sways on his feet. "I don't."

"I know."

One brow arches. "How do you know that?"

"Neighbors, remember?" No need to tell him I watch from my bedroom window all the time. He grins, and spears his fingers through his hair. "They didn't seem to like me very much," I add.

He shakes his head. "They don't like anyone."

"They really don't like you."

"No kidding. They blame me for..." He goes quiet—like he'd said too much already—and puts his hands over his head. He grips the door frame until his knuckles turn white. This is all very much a sore spot for him. I stand facing him in silence, the only audible sound in the room the coffee percolating. I want to ask about Cassie's mother—why she abandoned them, and if that's what his in-laws blame him for— but can't seem to bring myself to do it.

"I made coffee for you," I say. "I should get going."

I step toward the door he's occupying, expecting him to move, but he doesn't. Instead he stands there, his hands dropping to his sides, intense blue eyes trained on me. My God, he's the nicest looking man I ever set eyes on and I want him again.

"Last night," I begin. "That probably shouldn't have happened."

"But it did."

"It can't happen again."

"Why not?" There is a teasing edge to his voice. "You *are* my girlfriend."

I'm also trouble. Trouble he doesn't need in his life. If my ex ever came looking for me, no way would I want to bring that kind of danger into this household. Not that I don't think Jaxon can take care of himself. Of that I'm certain. But Cassie needs rainbows and butterflies, not crazy, jealous ex boyfriends who pose a danger. She's clearly been through enough already. So has Jaxon, judging by the pain ghosting his eyes.

"Jax—"

He presses his thumb to my lip, and warm sensations

travel all the way to the needy juncture between my legs. "Rach," he says. "I want you again. Tell me you don't want me, and I'll leave it at that. I swear to God, I'll never ask again."

I open my mouth to tell him I don't want him, but instead find myself saying, "I...I want you."

Oh, God how I want him.

He bends forward, presses warm lips to mine and my body instantly heats. He steps into me, his big hand going to the small of my back to anchor my body to his. His arousal presses against my stomach, and a whimper of need catches in my throat. I kiss him back, palm his body, but then a small working brain cell sounds alarm bells in the back of my brain, reminding me of my goals. It takes every ounce of strength I possess to break the kiss, and push back.

"We can't do this."

The heat in his eyes evaporates in an instant, and I don't know whether to laugh or cry, knowing he swore never to ask again. But nothing good could come from an affair with my neighbor, no matter how hot he is. He's trying hard to raise his daughter alone, and doesn't need the complication of me, or the baggage I bring. Plus, I think he's still hung up on his ex. As for me, I need to focus on school and keep a low profile.

"Okay," he says, and steps aside to clear a path for me.

Feeling the need to explain, I hesitate, and wring my hands together, "We need to keep things platonic between us." Karl's words ping around my brain. *She can't have people coming and going from her life. It's not healthy.* "I don't want Cassie to get attached or think there is more going on between us than there is. I'm not looking to fill her mother's shoes."

"You're absolutely right," he says.

6

JAXON

She was right.

She was absolutely fucking right, but that doesn't mean I have to like it. Taking Rachel to my bed was a mistake, but fuck, man, I can't stop thinking about her. Still, I can't let Cassie get attached to anyone, and hadn't planned to introduce any random women into her life.

Rachel's not random.

Fuck me. She might be my neighbor, but she has secrets, and that should be enough for me to keep my distance. But I can't help but feel protective of her, want to take care of her like she's mine.

She's not yours, dude.

With that last thought in mind, I grab the blow-up pool from the shed out back and shake it out, wanting to have it ready for when Cassie returns. Yeah, it's not an expensive below ground like her grandparents have, but we like it well enough.

The light flicks on in Rachel's room and I glance up. She's at work tonight. I saw her leave earlier, so I can only assume it's one of her roommates invading her privacy. The window inches up and I avert my gaze, my concentration going back to filling the pool. I feel a set of eyes on me as I work, but I ignore them, because the only eyes I want on me are Rachel's.

The night air is warm, sticky as I fill the pool with cold tap water. Once done, I peel off my shirt, and pants, and climb in in my boxers, the need to cool my body down having little to do with the heat wave.

I grab the beer I cracked earlier, and take a long pull from the bottle. Music starts up in the sorority house beside me. Another night, another party. Stretching out, I lean back against the rubber and watch the stars.

I sit in the pool for a good long time, the house beside me lit up with laughter and drinking. Will Rachel get any sleep tonight? Maybe I should go over there and tell them all to knock it off. I scoff. It's not really my place and since Rachel isn't mine, I shouldn't feel so protective of her.

After a long while, I climb from the pool, grab my clothes and step inside my house, which feels so lonely with Cassie at her grandparents. I peel off my boxers, and drop all my clothes into the basket near the washing machine. Walking through the house naked, my mind once again turns to Rachel, and I'm instantly hard. Fuck. I grip my cock, run my hands along the long length of it, and visualize it's Rachel touching me. I glance at the clock, and since I pretty much know her work shift, I step into my room, wanting to catch a glimpse of her. Christ, I must be some sort of masochist.

The lights are on when she enters, and I stand in the dark, stark naked, watching her like I'm some kind of pervert. Okay, this is wrong. I'm about to turn, draw the blinds and put on a pair of pants when a movement behind Rachel draws my focus. What the fuck? She's in there with some other guy? In the two months she's lived across from me, she's never had a guy in her room. Why now? Sending me a message that it really is over between us. Fuck, I got it the first time, Rach. No need to rub it in.

Despite that, I have an uneasy feeling prowling through my blood. Call it gut instinct, but something about all this isn't sitting right with me. I inch my window up to hear them talking, but the scream that comes from Rachel's mouth, and the sound of glass breaking sets me into motion. I grab my jeans and tug them on as I race down the hall and dash from the house. College students are hanging off the front deck as I hurry up the stairs two at a time and step into the house.

"Jaxon," I hear some girl squeal as I shove people out of my way and make quick work of the stairs. I burst through the closed door leading to Rachel's bedroom and quickly take in the scene unfolding before me. Rage takes hold of me and I grab the drunk asshole who has his hands all over Rachel as she fights him off.

He stumbles around, his eyes glassy and dilated as he smirks at me. "What the fuck are you doing, dude? Wait your turn."

In that moment, all I see is red. I grab the douche-bag by the collar and pull my hand back, ready to show him he's messing with the wrong girl. *My girl.* I'm about to knock him out cold, but Rachel's frightened scream stops me. She's almost hysterical as she backs up, and sits on her bed, her pillow in front of her like it's some sort of protection.

What the hell?

Understanding she needs me more than I need to knock this guy's head off, I shove him out the door, close it behind myself and start toward Rachel.

She holds her hands up, and her voice is bordering on hysteria when she says, "Don't come any closer."

My feet crunch on glass, and I back up to see a picture frame smashed on the floor. I pick it up, and my heart trips up when I look at the freckled face little girl in photo, and a woman who can only be her mother. But the picture is damaged from the broken glass.

"Rachel," I begin. "It's ruined. I'm sorry."

"Jaxon, please. Just leave."

"I'm not leaving. You're not okay. That guy almost—" I carefully set the photo and broken glass on her nightstand, and her face is pale as she looks at it. I somehow get the sense that it might just be the only picture of her and her mom.

"I know what that guy almost did," she says.

"It's not safe for you here." I grip a fistful of my hair. "Sleep at my place tonight." She opens her mouth, likely about to protest and I say, "Take the spare room." I take a step toward her, but she gives a hard shake of her head.

"No. Don't."

I go still, take in the tension in her posture, the way she's protecting herself with her pillow. "Rachel, what the fuck. I'm not going to hurt you."

"I need you to go, okay."

I take a few deep breaths, to calm myself. What the fuck is going on? She's acting like I'm the bad guy in this situation. Jesus fuck, some guy must have done one hell of a number on her. My insides boil, wanting to kill the bastard that had made her frightened of me. So help me if any guy from her past had laid a mean hand on her, I'll fucking kill him. That'll really give the sorority girls something to talk about.

Unable to let this go until I get to the bottom of matters, I inch back and change tactics, wanting the open Rachel from last night back. Then again, we were both so lust drunk, neither of us were in our right mind.

"Rach—"

She points to her door. "Leave, Jaxon. I want to be alone."

I reluctantly look at the door, note that it doesn't have a lock. Fuck. Any one of these assholes could come in here and try to attack her. I should pick her up and take her to my place whether she likes it or not. But that would only frighten her more.

"I'm right next door," I say and point to her window. "Yell out to me if you need me, or text, and I'll be here in two seconds."

"I'll be fine."

I glance around her room, and pick up her desk chair. "At least put this under the knob." It wasn't much but it was enough to keep those douche-bags out.

"Okay, I will."

She stands. I hand her the chair, and step out into the hall, closing her door behind me. I wait to hear her secure the chair under the door and turn to give a warning glare to every male in the vicinity. Message received, they clear a wide path as I stomp through the house, the fucker who tried to assault Rachel nowhere to be found. Good thing. I'd like to beat the shit out of him, but in the end, no good could come from that

I head home, and with my adrenaline pumping, I'm unable to wind down. I pace, flick the TV on and off again. I open the fridge and search for a beer, but I drank the last one earlier.

Fuck this.

Knowing there isn't a guy in the house next door who'd dare touch Rachel after my warning glare, I grab my keys, tug on my leather jacket and helmet, and head outside. With the night air so warm, I opt for my motorcycle instead of my car, and climb on. A good hard ride, and a good fuck are the only two things that are going to get my mind off Rachel. I rev the bike, loudly, and glance up when I catch her watching me from her room. I have no idea what I did to make her so angry with me, but she's on the run and obviously frightened by violence. I'm a guy with a violent past and that's where I need to keep it, or risk losing my daughter.

I pull out of my driveway, ease into traffic, and make my way to Jericho's, the pub I rarely get to anymore, but used to hang out at every weekend before Cassie was born. Do I miss it? Yeah, but I wouldn't change my life for the world. Cassie means everything to me and I'd give up breathing for her. I ease my bike between two big trucks and set the kickstand. Music blares from the open windows of the pub as I walk to the double doors. If push them open, and enter, keeping my back to the wall as I glance around. The smell of stale beer, smoke, and cheap perfume swirl around me, and I grin when I catch my buddies playing pool in the corner. Not much had changed over the years.

"Look what the fucking cat dragged in," Jericho, my friend and owner of the pub says, as he spreads his arms wide.

"Jericho, long time." I embrace him and we pat each other on the back as we hug in that typical man way. "Bet you could use a beer or two."

"Or two," I say. We part and he gestures to the waitress for another round.

"You here looking for trouble?" Sam asks, as he gives me that lopsided grin that has women dropping their panties. I glance at the pretty blonde on his arm. In the past we would have double-teamed, but those days are behind me.

"Just looking for a beer and a game," I say, as he puts his hand on my shoulder and gives it a welcoming squeeze.

"Missed you, bud."

"Like the Cleveland Browns miss a touchdown?"

He laughs. "Yeah, just like that. Rack 'em up," Sam says and gives his girl a whack on the ass to set her in to motion. "It's been far too long since I've taken your money," he ribs.

"Fuck you," I shoot back and we both laugh. A couple of other guys join us, and we shoot the shit as Sam's girl racks the balls. We flip for a break and I go first, sinking two low balls. I miss my third shot. No surprise considering I'm still shaken up over the incident at Rachel's.

I step back and give Sam the table. Jericho moves in beside me and I take a long pull from my bottle. He nudges me with his shoulder. "How did you manage to get out tonight?"

"In-laws have Cassie."

"Back from their trip?"

I nod and watch Sam sink two high balls. His girl presses her breasts to him and gives him a kiss with the promise of so much more to come. "Yeah."

He nods, a slow easy movement of his head, a good indication that he's got something other than Cassie and my in-laws on his mind. "Cassie's good?"

I smile. "Yeah, she's great."

"No news from Sarah."

"Not in a year." Not since I hired a private detective to find her, and had her served. She'd called me and threatened to take Cassie away if I went through with the divorce proceedings, but it was the only way I could move forward with my life—not that I've been doing a great job of that. I begged her to get clean and come home for her child's sake. Having Sarah in our lives again might not be the best for me, but I thought seeing her daughter again—seeing she is everything—would be enough to help her get clean.

"Then what's got you so fucking twisted up?"

Shit. Leave it to Jericho to see right through me. "Nothing," I say but I know him well enough to know he's not going to let it go.

He takes a drink from his bottle, holds it between his fingers and dangles it by his legs. "Okay, who is she, then?"

I angle my head slowly, and take in Jericho's concerned look. He really is one of the good guys and always had my back growing up. We go way back, which is why he can read me so well. Deciding there is no sense in trying to hide anything from him I shake my head and ask, "That obvious, huh?"

"We haven't seen you in a month, and you show up here looking like you want to kill someone."

"That's because I do."

He cracks his knuckles. "Point the way."

I scoff, and put my hand on my friend's shoulder. "Those days are behind me. No good can come from me fighting. The in-laws would use that against me, and I can't risk losing Cassie. She's everything."

"And the girl who's got you fucked up?"

"Neighbor. Fixing her car. Some college douche-bag tried to assault her tonight."

"Fuck, man, and you didn't kill him."

"Wanted to." I grab the chalk and run it over the end of my cue.

"You serious about her."

"No. It's nothing. Just a one-night thing."

"You're not acting like it's nothing."

"Well it is," I shoot back.

"K, then." He rubs the dark scruff on his chin, and I glance at his tattooed knuckles as he calls over a hot brunette in daisy dukes. "Wanda is just the girl to help you get your mind off things."

"Not interested."

Fuck, man. Any other time I'd have taken him up on the offer and banged Wanda in the back room. Rachel has gotten under my skin more than I care to admit.

Jericho deep rumble of laughter reverberates through me. He pats me on the back. "Yeah, that's what I thought."

Motherfucker.

RACHEL

Rachel

Another Saturday, another nasty customer.

Honest to God I need to quit this job. Then again, it's not like I can blame the customer for being pissed off. They waited forever for their pizza, only for me to screw the order up. They asked for no olives and I gave them an all-olive pizza. Well done, Rachel, well done. Goddammit, if I don't get my head in the game, I'm going to lose this job. Not that the pay or hours are stellar, but it comes with a steady paycheck and I need that. I'll quit when I find a new job— not that I have the time to look for one. So, for now this is it, and I need to get my shit together.

I avoid my boss as I untie my apron, and shove it into my backpack. He yelled at me twice tonight already and from the look on his face, I'd say he wants to go for a hat trick. I clock out, grab the pepperoni pizza I'd made and just paid for, and dart outside, desperate to breathe in the warm night air. I stand still for one moment to think about my past, my present and my future. A seed of worry moves through me and when the hair on my arms tingle, like I'm being watched, I wrap one arm around myself and hug. No way can Dylan know where I am, right? Then again, it could be the creepy customer who hits on me every chance he gets. I do another quick scan of the streets only to find them empty of anyone threatening.

Everything will be fine, Rachel.

After quickly lecturing myself, I hurry home, and hear the music long before I take the corner and see my house lit up. Once again my mind races to Jaxon, and the way he came to my rescue. I cringe inwardly. I might have been scared when that asshole was mauling me, but the anger on Jaxon's face not only frightened me, it took me back to a violent place I never want to go again. In that moment, all I could see was images of Dylan holding a baseball bat over his head and threatening to kill me if I left him.

But all Jaxon was doing was trying to protect me, right? His anger wasn't aimed at me. Maybe not, but it was still unleashed anger, and that kind of uncontrolled rage scares the hell out of me. I breathe deep, and a little sound escapes my throat when I recall the pained look in his Jaxon's eyes when I told him to leave. It shouldn't bother me as much as it does. We agreed to a once night of sex only affair, and there was no need for him to run to my rescue.

But there is a part of me that is touched by the gesture. Warmed by it. Sure, my ex was domineering and possessive. Jaxon obviously has the same traits. If I got involved with him deeper, would those qualities eventually turn him into a mean, control freak, and end with me on the run again?

There is a part of me that doesn't think so.

But then again, there is a part of me that warns never to get close to a guy like that again. I reach my front door, and can't help but steal a glance toward Jaxon's bedroom. The light is off. In fact, his entire place looks dark. Perhaps he took off on his bike again, like he did last night after I blatantly told him to leave me alone.

I push through the front door and Val is standing there, drink in hand, with a big smirk on her face.

"So I take it you and slurpalicious have done the deed."

"Don't call him that," I say, suddenly on the defense.

Beer sloshes over her red cup as she takes another drink. "Oh, and why not? You hot for him?"

Of course I'm hot for him, but she doesn't need to know that.

"Because he's more than just a body. He's a father, and a good guy."

A really nice guy.

I stomp past her, and climb the stairs, pushing my way through the drunken horde of freshmen. I take two steps toward my room and stop dead in my tracks, my heart jumping into my throat.

What the hell?

I blink, sure I'm hallucinating. But when I open my eyes again, the vision of Jaxon installing a lock on my door dances before my eyes.

"What are you doing?" I ask, even though it's obvious.

His body stiffens and he doesn't even spare me a glance when he answers with, "What does it look like I'm doing?"

"Ah, putting a lock on my door."

"Then you have your answer," he says, not a hint of warmth in his voice. He's pissed at me, yet he's still here putting a lock on my door for *my* safety. I swallow past a gritty throat, my knees a little less stable then they were a second ago. As he twists a screwdriver, I stand still. Shit, I don't even know what to say about this. He shoves the tool into his back pocket, reaches for my free hand, and presses a key into it. "There is a deadbolt for when you're in your room, and a lock on the outside for when you're not home. No one, not even your roommates, will be able to get in when you're not here."

I open my palm, look at the new silver key. My heart does a little somersault. "I..."

"Step inside." he commands in a rough tone. I walk past him, but he continues to avoid eye contact with me. I step into my room, set my pizza on my dresser, and he closes my door, slamming it shut with a little more force than necessary. I practically jump out of my shoes. "Lock it," he grumbles. I slide the deadbolt in to place and wait. "Locked?" he asks.

"Yes." He wiggles the knob, and I step back.

"Now you're safe. No assholes will be bothering you again."

"Thank you," I say quietly.

I wait for a moment. Is he going to ask me to open the door again? If he does what the hell do I say to him? I'm so thrown off by this sweet gesture, I'm a bit speechless, and that's not normal for me.

I step back up to the door, press my ear to it. "Jaxon," I whisper. Is he on the opposite side of the wooden panel, with his ear pressed to the wood? I wait, and when no response comes, I say his name louder, to be heard over the music. Seconds turn into minute and I suck in a fueling breath. Obviously, we need to talk. I slide the deadbolt, and inch open my door, only to find the hall empty. I back up, and plunk myself on my bed. Goddammit, why does he have to be so sweet?

I pick up my phone and, and pull up his contact information. Should I text him? If I do am I sending the wrong message. I don't want him to get the idea that I want more from him, but I need to make things right between us. He didn't deserve to be treated the way I treated him last night.

I stand and walk to my window. The lights in his place are still off. I lift my window, lean out and catch a glimpse of him in his backyard. I peer into the night, the moon providing sufficient light for me to see him strip down to his boxers and climb into the pool. I stifle a laugh as he squeezes his big body into the blow-up rubber ring.

The scent of my pizza hits me, and I walk to my dresser. I pick it up, step from my room and head out into the night. I walk quietly to the back of Jaxon's house and find him kicking back in the water with a cold beer in his hands.

"Hey," I say.

His body stiffens, his beer dangling from his fingertips. "What can I do for you, Rachel?" he asks.

I step in front of him, giving him no choice but to face me. I hold the pizza out. "Peace offering."

He goes quiet, too quiet, his blue eyes trained on my face. I suck in a breath and hold it, as I wait for his response. He finally breaks the quiet.

"Pepperoni?"

"And extra cheese."

He sits forward, and water splashes around his thighs. My eyes dip, take in his wet boxers, the way they're clinging to his body, one part in particular.

He scrubs his chin. "You don't play fair."

"All is fair in love and war," I counter, and open the box.

"So what is this, love or war?"

Good question. "It's friendship. I don't want war between us, Jaxon, and I owe you an apology. I overreacted, and I'm sorry."

The lines around his mouth soften, and I revel in the sight of his lips, remember the way his mouth felt on my body.

Glorious.

I set the box down on the picnic table, and hand him a

slice, but when I do, he grabs me, gives a little tug, and I end up falling into the rubber pool with an undignified thud.

"Jaxon," I yelp and brush my wet hair from my face. "What are you doing?"

"You looked hot."

"Now my clothes are all wet."

"Take them off."

"Not likely."

He shrugs. "Leave them on then." He takes a huge bite of the pizza. "This is delicious. Did you make it?" He turns the slice around for me to take a bite. I hesitate for a second. I've never shared a slice with anyone before and it kind of feels...intimate.

Then again, nothing is more intimate than what we did last night in his bed, right? I take a bite, and Jaxon brings it back to his mouth.

I chew, swallow and say, "I made it before I left work."

"Damn, maybe I'll have to visit Pizza Villa."

"Try to do it on a night when I'm off. I screwed up a few orders tonight. The boss wasn't very happy with me."

His face goes serious, protector mode. Honest to God the man really is a warrior. "Want me to have a little talk with him?"

I laugh. "No, Jaxon. I'm a big girl and can take care of myself and I can't lose this job."

He lifts his bottle to my mouth. "Drink," he says.

I take a pull from the bottle and let the cold beer wash the pizza down. He drinks after me and I wipe my mouth. "Thanks." He finishes the slice, leans out of the pool, and with a long stretch, grabs another. He offers me the first bite.

We both go quiet as we eat, lost in our own thoughts. Jaxon is a nice guy, and a great father. We'd only just really met, and I don't want tension between us. We are, after all neighbors—who can see into each other's windows. And we have to be around each other since I offered my services for fixing my car. Truthfully, I can't back out of it, because I just don't have the money to pay him.

I finally break the quiet and say, "Are we okay?"

"Yeah, we're okay." He leans toward me, and nudges my chin with his fist, his warm breath washing over my face. "I just need you to know something." I go quiet and wait to hear what he says as he tugs on his hair and shakes his head. "I'd never hurt you, Rachel. I might have beaten that asshole to within an inch of his life, but I'd never lay a hand on you."

I look down as my heart crashes against my chest. It's just so hard for me to trust, but I'm not about to get into my personal life with a man I barely know. Than another thought hits. "I'm not worth the fight, Jaxon." He opens his mouth like he's about to protest, but I continue with, "You have a little girl and fighting won't look good to the courts. If your in-laws ever found out, they could use that against you."

Callused fingers cup my chin, and nudge it upward until we're eye to eye. "I don't know who the guy from you past is, and you don't have to tell me anything, but goddammit, Rachel, he did a number on you, and if I ever got my hands on him..." His voice trails off.

My heart misses a beat. "How do you know about—"

He shakes his head and cuts me off. "I'm not him. I won't lay a hand on you, Rachel." I take in the blue of his eyes, the way they drop to my mouth like he's dying for a taste. He clears his throat and adds, "Unless, of course you want me to."

I swallow. Hard. I left his house with the intentions of never touching him again and he told me once I said no to being with him sexually, he'd never ask. But the truth is, I want him again. I want to feel his arms around me. Want to feel his naked body next to mine. Just one more time.

"Jaxon," I whisper, even though what I'm doing isn't smart or rational. This man has obviously put the pieces of my life together and figured out a thing or two about me when I was trying to stay under the radar.

"Yeah."

"I want you to."

He takes in a huge breath, holds it for a moment, then exhales slowly. "Are you sure, Rachel? I need you to be—"

I press my fingers to his lips and shift until I'm sitting on his lap. When he stops speaking, I place my hands on either side of his face, and instead of answering with words, I lower my lips to his. I open for him, and welcome his tongue. The deep groan that catches in his throat sings through me and arouses me even more. I want this. I want him. Right here, right now, in this moment. That's the only thing I care about —and I can't say that's a good thing.

He slides his arms around my back, and drags me closer, my breasts pressing against his wet chest as he centers his erection against my core, a good indication that he *wants* this, too.

He holds me to him as he pushes from the pool and stands, and I wrap my legs around his back to hold on. From the east side of my house, where anyone can see into Jaxon's backyard, a chorus of whistles reaches our ears. Jaxon breaks the kiss, a scowl on his face. "I think we'd better take this inside."

"Yeah, good idea."

"But first this." He turns to glare at the guys whistling. "Just so you fuckers know. She's mine and if you lay one hand on her or even look at her the wrong way, I'll beat the living fuck out of every single one of you."

Nervous laughter fills the air, but from the way the group of freshmen are backing away from the side of the house, their voices lowering, it's clear every drunk frat boy partying at my place has received Jaxon's message loud and clear. Maybe they're not so stupid after all.

He looks back at me. "I'm sorry, Rach. You don't like violence, I get that, but no one is touching you when you're with me, and no one is looking. I'm not sharing any part of you with those assholes, or anyone else."

My heart pinches at his possessive behavior. Oddly enough, I'm not afraid this time. I actually feel cocooned in bubble of warmth and safety as he holds me close and displays the domineering side of him.

I shiver and he must mistake it for being cold. "Let's get you inside and out of these wet clothes." He takes the steps up to the back patio, and opens the sliding door. I quiver again when he sets the lock, blocking out the rest of the world.

"Warm shower?" he asks.

I run my fingers through my damp hair. I really could use a shower to wash the marinara out. "As long as the tap doesn't come off and I end up with a cold one again," I say, and give a nervous little laugh. I'm not sure why I suddenly feel so edgy. We had sex two nights ago, but it's oddly weird how this feels different...a little more personal. Maybe it's because of the fight. Maybe it brought us closer in some way.

Or maybe I'm just being ridiculous and reading more into this when I shouldn't be.

This is sex, Rachel. Nothing more, nothing less.

He angles his head, like he can see right through me. "You okay?"

"I am," I say, and inch up to kiss him on the mouth. We're both breathless when we finally break apart and he sets me on the kitchen table.

"I fixed the tap today." He steps back. "Arms up."

I do as he says and he peels off my ugly brown T-shirt. Air rushes over my bare skin, and I tremble. Jaxon's nostrils flare as I sit before him in my bra and pants. "You did?"

"Yeah, I didn't want you taking any more cold showers."

"So you were pretty sure that I was going to use your shower again, I take it."

He grins. "Not really, but just in case."

He reaches behind me to unlatch my bra. "Well, that was very thoughtful of you," I say quietly.

His lids fall slowly, then lift again to reveal eyes that are just a little darker than before. "I don't always think about myself, you know," he informs me, but there is a teasing warmth behind his words, one that tells me the conversation has shifted to something a little more...intimate.

Truthfully though, he doesn't have to tell me that he's not selfish. I've seen him with his daughter, and he jumped to help me when my car broke down. "I know you don't always think about yourself."

His chin raises, and hungry blue eyes meet mine as he releases the button on my pants. "Sometimes I do, though. Sometimes I think only about myself."

My nerves fire, come to life under his ravenous gaze. "You do?"

"Yeah."

I wet my suddenly dry bottom lip. "So tell me, when you're thinking about yourself, what exactly are you thinking about?"

He lifts me from the table, drops to his knees and drags my pants down my thighs. My entire body vibrates when the backs of his knuckles skate over my skin, his hairs abrading my flesh. He stands, and the rough pad of his thumb brushes my swollen clit through my panties.

"Lately, I've been thinking about this," he says, and slides my panties down until my sex is exposed. He goes to his knees again, taps my leg and I lift both feet, one at a time, allowing him to remove the rest of my clothes.

"This?" I ask and arch my brows. "You might have to be more specific. *This* can refer to a number of things."

He widens my sex with his fingers, and strokes my clit. "Right here, Rachel. I've been thinking about your hot pussy, and all the things I want to do with it."

"O...ohh," I say, shivers of need making it a bit hard to stay upright. I brace one hand on the table to keep myself vertical. He stands and I moan, my sex desperate for his touch. "I've also been thinking about this." He brushes his thumb over my bottom lip, then shoves it inside like he did the last time we were alone. I suck him in, swirl my tongue around the rough pad. Our eyes latch and lock, the heat between us tremendous.

He pulls out and his tortured, needy growl reaches my ears and urges me on. "You've been thinking about putting your thumb into my mouth again?" I tease.

"No. I want my cock in here," he says, his words blunt, and unapologetic. "This mouth of yours is sinful and I want you to suck me off while I fuck it, Rachel. I want to be buried balls-fucking-deep in your throat when I shoot a load off." His breathing changes, becomes labored, and his nostrils flare like he's a bull ready for the stampede. "I want you to take me in, all of me, and I want you to swallow every fucking drop of my cum. Then I want to take you everywhere, fuck every sweet inch of you. That's what goes through my mind when I'm being selfish," he adds.

It takes a minute for my lust-drunk brain to catch up, absorb all his dirty thoughts. Holy God! I might be in over my head with this guy. *You already knew that, Rachel.* Despite that, I drop to my knees, and say, "I think you should be selfish more often."

"What are you doing?" he asks and grips my hair.

I tug on his boxers, and his hard cock pops free. "Mmm," I moan, never more eager to pleasure a man orally. Honest to God, knowing this is what he thinks about, fantasizes about... well, that's a complete turn on.

The grip on my hair tightens, as I lean forward and take him to the back of my throat. I choke a bit, and he tugs like wants to inch out, give me air, but the hell with that. I want him to choke me. I want to take him as deep as I can, and then some. Yeah, I get that I can't take all of him. He's too big for that, but dammit, I'm going to do my best to fulfill all his selfish needs.

"Rach," he says, his voice soft when I choke again. Undeterred, I loosen my throat muscles and slide him down farther. He stretches me, but I love every second of it. Truthfully, I've never taken any man so deep, and from the way Jaxon is growling, cursing, jerking his hips and gripping my hair, I'm guessing this is a first for him, too. Knowing that fills me with female prowess, because strangely enough, I want to do a lot of first things with my hot neighbor.

"Jesus, fuck," he grumbles, and I cup his balls, massage gently. They tighten in my hands, and I work my mouth over him fast, my free hand gripping his base and moving in tandem with my hungry mouth. Pre-cum spurts from his crown, and I swallow the salty tang. I inch back slightly, to release the moan caught in my throat. My needy little sounds seem to make Jaxon a little bit needier.

"You've got the nicest fucking mouth," he says and moves my hair from my face, to watch his cock slide in and out of it. "I'm right there, Rachel. I going to fill your throat with my cum if you don't back off."

I secretly smile, and slide one hand around his ass to stop him from escaping. I rock against him, and he in turn rocks in to me. Never in my life had I wanted to please a man so badly, to make this so good for him. He gives up on trying to pull out, and when I feel blood rushing through his swollen veins, I go still.

"Yessss..." he growls and lets go, his hot seed filling my mouth and throat. I keep my mouth open for him, and gulp and swallow, wanting every drop of him inside me. His breathing is rough and ragged and he clutches my head with both of his hands to keep me from moving. He continues to spurt, and I continue to swallow, until he's completely depleted, and panting hard

"Rach, holy fuck, Rach," he finally says, and drops to his knees in front of me. "I can't...I don't even..." His dark gaze rakes over my face, his eyes puzzled, perplexed. "That was... Jesus." He runs shaky fingers over my mouth to wipe away the moisture.

My pulse beats triple time against my neck. I love seeing him unglued like this. "Sometimes it's fun to be selfish," I tell him.

"Yeah but you didn't have to—"

I press my finger to his lips. "Did you ever stop to think I was being selfish, too? That I might lay in bed and think about how much I'd like to have your cock in my mouth."

He blinks, and his head goes back like he's in total disbelief. "You've got to be kidding me."

"Would I kid about something like that?"

"I just...never thought..."

"I loved you fucking my mouth, Jaxon."

He exhales slowly and shakes his head. "You're really... wow...I've never met a woman like you, Rach."

"Since we're being honest, I should probably let you know, there are other things I think about too when I'm being selfish."

He dips his head, the bewildered look gone from his face, deep seated lust moving in to take its place. "Tell me," he demands in a soft voice.

He shimmies closer to me, and his cock flinches against my stomach. I gasp, hardly able to believe he's getting hard for me again so soon. He just came in my mouth. Is this what I do to him?

"I think about your mouth on my body, kissing me every-where, and your fingers, well, they're always on me...inside me...totally corrupting me and turning me into one of those dim-witted moths like my roommates." A fine quiver moves through me, and Goosebumps break out on my skin.

Before I even realize what's going on, I'm in his arms and he's stomping down the hallway. He steps into the bathroom, kicks the door shut behind us, and sets me on the counter. I chuckle when he steps away from me, and turns on the hot water.

"Something funny?" he grumbles.

I point to his wet shorts, which are still around his thighs. How could he even walk with them like that? "I was in a hurry," he says and kicks them off. "When a girl tells you she wants your mouth on her and your fingers inside, you don't stop to worry about anything else." He crooks his fingers. "Now get over here, so I can corrupt you."

I slide off the counter, my body so eager and ready for this man. Maybe too eager, too ready. It's almost a bit scary how much I want him.

He ushers me into the shower, lets the hot water pour over my body, then spins me around until I'm facing the back tiled wall. He slides a foot between my feet and a needy little whimper catches in my throat as he widens my legs. He puts his mouth near my ear, his breath hot on my neck, and my body fires when he whispers, "Don't even think about closing them."

I shiver at the warning, the way he's taking command of my body. By rights, it should frighten me, but I only feel safe in his arms. He runs his fingers down my arms, and captures both of my hands. "If you want me to corrupt you, then we're doing things my way tonight," he whispers, as he takes my hands, splays my palms, and presses them into the wall.

I whimper, never having felt so wide open to anyone before. "Jaxon," I murmur.

"Just like that, Rach. Wide open and mine to ruin."

My chest heaves as he slides a hand around my waist, pulling me back a bit from the wall. As I tip my ass to him, my hands slide a little lower on the wet tile. The scent of his soap reaches my nostrils as he lathers it in his hands, and the wait is pure freaking torture.

"Touch me..." I whisper, a desperate sort of plea that pulls a chuckle from him.

"Aren't you a needy girl? Anxious to have my hands on you." He puts his mouth near my ear again. "My hard cock in you."

"Yes," I say without hesitation or embarrassment. What has this man turned me in to?

"I shouldn't make you wait, not after the way you sucked my cock, worshipped it. You should be fucking rewarded for that." He places his hands on my back, and the leans into me as he reaches for my tits. "Oh yeah, you should be given anything you want after letting me fuck your mouth like that."

I swallow, and I'm sure I'm going to climax from his dirty words alone. "Jaxon," I moan and arch into his touch as he swipes his thumbs over my nipples. The pleasure travels through my body, pulses between my shaky legs.

"Do you have any idea how good you are with that sweet mouth of yours?"

"No," I say. With my ex, there was never a lot of foreplay. It was just sex, him taking what he wanted, fast and furious. "It's not something I normally..."

Oh, God, way to admit your lack of experience, Rachel.

"You did that just for me, Rach." His voice is so damn soft, and surprised, my heart tightens a little. For a big scary guy, probably the toughest guy I know, he sure knows how to pluck at my emotional strings.

"Yeah. Just for you."

He goes quiet for a moment, and I move my hips, needing to get my mind back on my body—the pleasure his cock can give—and off the emotions this guy brings out in me.

Big hands go to my hips, and slide over my ass. "Does your hot little pussy need my fingers?" From behind, he pushes his hand between my legs, and strokes my clit.

"Yes...." I murmur, and move with him, rearing back and jerking forward as he plays with me.

"You're so wet. I think you need to come."

"I do," I practically scream, and he chuckles. "It's not funny."

"Not funny at all." One big finger fills me and I give a moan of relief. "This what you need?"

"It is," I manage to say. He pulls out, then slides a second finger in. I grip at the wall and try to get air in my lungs.

"After you come for me, do you think you can take my cock? I'm so fucking hard again."

He wiggles his fingers inside of me, and I whimper. How is he so good at that? Then again, maybe I don't want to know. Maybe last night when he blew out of here, he was meeting up with some woman. But that thought is for another time, when I'm not being finger-fucked.

"Can I have your cock now?"

"Can't."

"Please, Jaxon."

"Fuck, girl. I want that too, but I don't have a condom in here."

"I'm on the pill, and I'm clean." His fingers stop moving, and need fills me. "Jaxon?"

"I'm clean too, Rach. I've not been with anyone in a long time."

A little thrill goes through me. "If we're both clean, and I'm on the pill, then we can fuck right now," I say.

"Yeah, I guess we can." He removes his fingers and I practically scream hallelujah when he presses his crown to my pussy. "This is what you want?"

"Yes."

"You want to come all over my cock?"

"Jaxon," I groan. "I need your cock now."

His hands go to my waist, and his fingers bite into my skin as he powers forward.

"Ohmigod," I cry out as he fills me in a way I've never been filled before. He pulls me off the wall, runs his hands over my breasts as he seats himself high inside.

"Fuck girl, you feel good."

"So good," I cry out and rotate my hips.

"Oh, yeah, keep doing that."

I move my body some more, squeeze my sex muscles around the hard length of him. The man just came, but he's hard and swollen, his next orgasm just around the corner, judging by the way he's swelling inside me. He's not the only one who's close. He isn't even moving, and small clenches are pulling at me. I lean forward again, press my hands to the wall, and offer myself up to him.

A quiver moves through me as he slides out, only to slam back in again. "Fuck me," I whimper, as he powers home. We moved together, lovers in sync, creating a rhythm and harmony that pushes me to the edge. I cling there, wanting to hang on, revel in each glorious thrust, but I can't. I close my eyes, soar over the edge, and squeeze hard around his cock.

"Oh, yesss..." I cry out and the grip on my hips tightens as I release.

"Yeah, Rach. Come for me. Come all over my cock." He rocks into me, drawing out each blissful clench. I grasp at the wall, breathe through the pleasure until I'm wrung out and sated. Jaxon leans over me, presses open-mouthed kisses to my back as he releases again. His hot cum spurts high inside me, warming me from the inside out.

"So good," he murmurs against my skin.

He pulls me from the wall again, presses his mouth to my neck. "Stay with me tonight," he whispers.

I open my mouth to say no—any more time in his arms will be emotional suicide at best—but the only word to come out of my mouth is...yes.

JAXON

Jaxon

The coolness in the air pulls me awake, and I open one eye to see Rachel snuggled next to me, hogging all the blankets. She's wrapped up tighter than a burrito and it brings a smile to my face. I move closer, roll her a bit and tug on the blanket to slide under it with her. She shimmies backward toward me and as we spoon, I absorb her heat. She moans to let me know she's awake.

"I think the heat wave is over," I say quietly.

I get a one-word murmured reply of, "Good."

"Why good?" Body still chilled, I shiver and slide my hand down her thigh.

"No way will I get any studying done with you hanging out in your pool in nothing but your boxers."

"I'm a distraction, am I?"

"Big time."

I laugh. "So when you say big...?"

She laughs with me, rolls over and whacks me with her pillow. "Ego much?

I grab the pillow, toss it away and capture both her hands. Her eyes go wide as I pin her to the bed and climb over her.

Her body softens beneath me, and my cock swells even more. Fuck, I can't get enough of her. I growl, desperate to slide high inside her again.

"Spread your legs," I say. "I want to fuck you."

"Jaxon," she murmurs, her eyes wide as a warm pink flush paints her cheek. "Didn't you get enough last night?"

I have no idea how many times we fucked last night. All I know is it was well into the wee hours of the morning when she fell asleep in my arms.

"No, did you?"

A smile curls the corners of her mouth. "No."

My insides soften, a tenderness overcoming me when I realize I'd been a bit rough with her. Fuck, there were times I went at her like a hormonal teen, a goddamn caveman. Insane really, considering I'm a grown-ass man who hasn't thought about sex—well, okay maybe a little—since my ex split. But this sweet woman in my bed does something to me. I run my thumb over her plump, kiss-swollen bottom lip, my mouth eager to be on hers again.

"Are you sore?"

"A little."

"Can you take me again?"

Her legs slide apart, and my heart hammers. I fucking love that she's so ready and eager

"You sure?" I ask, giving her once last chance out before I bury myself balls deep inside her.

"One hundred percent."

With my cock hard and ready, I press my crown to her opening and my lips find hers. I slide into her, slowly, and she moans into my mouth.

"You like that?" I ask quietly.

"Yeah," she murmurs and runs her hands over my body. I quiver as she touches me, palms my muscles like she's reacquainting herself with my body.

"I like the way you touch me," I say. As she continues her exploration, I move inside her, slower this time, less hurried, but from the way her eyes are slipping shut, it's clear she likes this every bit as much as she liked me taking her fast and furiously.

"I could wake up like this every morning," she murmurs, but then her eyes open. "I mean..."

"I know what you mean," I say. "I like fucking you too, Rach, and it got me thinking."

"About," she says, her hips lifting slightly to meet each slow thrust.

"Maybe we could keep doing this while I'm working on your car."

"Yeah?"

"Sure. I should finish the job in a week or so. Why don't we just keep enjoying each other until then." I increased the pace a tiny bit, and press hot kisses to her neck—a ploy to shut down her mind until only 'yes' is on her lips. "When the car is done, and you're no longer babysitting or cleaning for me, things go back to the way they were."

Her nails scratch at my back, and soft clenches squeeze my cock. "That sounds...oh, damn that's good."

"Is that a yes?" I ask.

"Yessss..." she cries out, but I'm pretty sure it has more to do with her orgasming around my cock than answering my question. Her hot cum singes my dick, and I grip her hair, drive into her once, twice, then go perfectly still as I fill her with my seed.

I breathe hard against her neck, my body no longer cold from the chill in the morning air. She hugs me to her and I collapse on top of her.

"How are you so good at this?" she asks, a bubble of laughter in her voice. "Honest to God, I've come more in the last twenty-four hours than I have in my entire life."

I lift my head to see her, and brush her hair from her face. I cup her cheeks and even though she hasn't agreed to my proposition yet, I say, "That's a goddamn shame and for the next two weeks, I'm going to be sure you come at least once a day."

She laughs. "I have school, work, and chores around here. How can you promise that?"

"If I have to come to your work and drag you into the bathroom for an orgasm, I'll do it."

Her eyes go wide as she sits up and rests against the backboard. "You wouldn't."

I slide my hands across the mattress, stroke her nipple. "Yeah, I would."

She whacks me. "You're just kidding. You would never do that?"

"Would I kid about something like that?" I say, tossing her playful words back at her.

"That would be a great way to get me fired," she says, but I don't miss the pleasure in her eyes.

"You sound like you like my idea."

"Well..."

"You need a new job."

"Yeah, no kidding?"

"What do you know about cars?" I tease. "I could always use help in the shop."

She gives me a wry look. "Believe me, you don't want me anywhere near your garage."

"You're right, too much of a distraction," I say, my stomach taking that moment to grumble.

"On that note, you'd better get some food into you, and I need to get home and hit the books."

"Let me cook you breakfast before you go." She glances at the clock, and crinkles her nose. "If you want, I can even teach you how to make pancakes from scratch."

She rolls her eyes at me. "I know how to cook. I was just in a hurry."

"I knew it."

"Knew what?"

"That you were trying to sneak out of here." She frowns, and plucks at the blankets. "Hey what?"

A moment of silence and then, "I don't want Cassie to get the wrong idea about us, Jaxon. I don't want her to think I'm anything more than her sitter, or your client. I can't be her mom figure."

I rake my fingers through my hair. "I know. I don't want you to be." She looks away for a moment, but I catch the conflicting emotions on her face before she turns. "Rach?"

"Yeah?"

"What?" I ask.

She turns back to me. "Where is her...mom?"

As anger and sadness move through me, I push from the bed, and walk to my closet. I grab a pair of jeans and tug them on.

"I'm sorry. Never mind. It's none of my business," she says quickly.

I turn, and Rachel's back is to me as she searches the floor for something to wear. She grabs my t-shirt from last night, and pulls it on. My heart misses a beat as she stands there in my clothes.

"She left us," I say. "We weren't enough for her."

Rachel stiffens and turns to me. "I'm sorry."

"She ran off with her dealer," I tell her. I'm not sure why I'm opening up. I keep that part of my life pretty confidential, and don't like to talk about it—with anyone. Not even the guys. When it comes right down to it, I'm private. That's a trait Rachel and I have in common. She's yet to tell me anything about herself, and I respect that. We're having a brief affair. Nothing more, nothing less. Her demons are hers, and mine are mine. But I still can't help but wonder...

"Ohmigod, Jaxon. I had no idea."

She steps up to me, slides her hands around my body and lays her cheek near my heart.

"Her parents don't know the extent of her drug addiction, and they blame me for her leaving," I say.

She lifts her chin, looks into my eyes. "How is it your fault?"

"When we met, we were both big into partying, but I slowed down and stopped her when she got pregnant. She couldn't handle this life I guess. She got deeper into the drug scene, then eventually left."

I run my fingers through her hair and hold her to me.

"Do you still love her?"

"She gutted me, Rach, and I hate what she did to Cassie, but I can't deny that I worry about her. She is, after all, the mother of my child."

Rachel presses her lips to my chest. "If she came back clean, you guys could be a family again," she says, her voice softer, lower than a minute ago.

"I really hope she gets herself clean, and gets her life back on track." Not because I want her back, but because Cassie needs her mother. "How about those pancakes?" I say, not wanting to dredge up any more painful memories.

She pushes from me and her smile is a bit wobbly. "Yeah, sure." She injects a lightness in her voice that doesn't quite reach her eyes.

I reach back into my closet and hand her a pair of my sweats. She climbs into them and masochistic bastard that I am, I watch her. My cock jumps in my jeans. Why the hell can't I get enough of her? I'm not sure but I'm hoping that over the course of the next couple weeks, I'll fuck her out of my system.

"Are you going to put on a shirt?" she asks.

"I wasn't going to." She plants her hands on her hips, the look so sexy my throat dries. "You want me to?"

"Yes, Jaxon. You really have to stop walking around half naked all the time."

"And here I was thinking you should do it more often. Especially when you're in your room and walking past your window."

She points to my dresser. "Get a shirt on. Now."

Laughing, I grab one and tug it on. "Better?"

"Yes."

She leaves the room and I follow her out. She darts into the bathroom and I head to the kitchen to put the coffee on. But first I pick her clothes up from the floor, a grin on my face as I recall the way I'd removed them from her body last night. I set them on the chair, flicked on some tunes, and start the pancake batter. That's when I realize I'm still smiling. Christ, I can't remember the last time a woman made me walk around my place grinning like the village idiot.

"I love that song," Rachel says, coming around the corner. She sways to the song, and grabs two mugs from the cupboard, already familiar with my kitchen, and I kind of like how she feels so at home.

"Chocolate chips or blueberries?" I ask as I dump flour into a bowl.

"Ah, chocolate," she says. "Like that should even be a question."

"You and Cassie. Am I going to have to try to sneak fruit into your meals, too?"

She goes up on her toes, and taking me by surprise, places the softest kiss on my mouth. "You're a good dad," she says and my heart misses a beat as she pours us each a steaming mug of java.

I dump a handful of chocolate chips into the batter, heat up the frying pan, and pour.

"Mmm, smells good."

I make a couple of pancakes quickly and Rachel grabs utensils and sits at the table as I divvy them up. I settle in next to her. We dig into our pancakes and both go a bit quiet, lost in thought as we eat.

"So you're studying for the rest of the day?" I ask after emptying my plate.

"Yeah, and I have a paper to write for my Humanities class. How about you?"

"I need to make some calls for your radiator. I've got a few leads, and since I didn't get to the grocery store yesterday, that means groceries, and getting lunches and meals planned for the week for Cassie."

She goes quiet, her eyes a bit solemn. "When was the last time you had fun?"

I take a big drink of my coffee. "I could ask you the same thing."

She slides her fork into her mouth, takes a look at the clock on the wall, and says, "Oh, about thirty minutes ago." We both laugh and I push back from the table. Rachel sets her fork down, and her eyes meet mine.

"How about we get out of here, go have some fun before I study and you work?" she asks.

"Yeah?"

"Sure, we could hit the outdoor market. I can help you get your groceries, and we can grab an ice cream or something."

"Or something?"

"Stop." She finishes her last bite of pancake, and says, "What time do you pick Cassie up?"

"Around dinner."

"Too bad. I'm sure she would have liked an ice cream, but

then again, it's best she not see us together and get the wrong idea, right?"

"Right."

She places her hands on the table and stands. "Okay, let's get the dishes done, then I'll get changed and meet you outside."

"I'll do the dishes." I nod toward the door. "You go on and get ready."

"Give me twenty," she says, and gathers her clothes up from the chair. She removes my sweats, and pulls on her work pants and darts outside.

I make quick work of the dishes, take a two-minute shower, and tug on a clean pair of jeans and a t-shirt.

The rising sun pushes back the chill of the night, and it's warm when I step outside. My gaze goes to Rachel's car. For the next two weeks while it's out of commission, I plan to drive her back and forth to campus. I have to take Cassie to school and it's not really out of my way.

My pulse jumps, so does one other body part, when she exits her house, looking so girl-next-door-fresh, it's all I can do not to drag her back to my bed. She darts a nervous glance up and down the street, her eyes searching—for what or who I don't know. All I do know is that someone has hurt her, left her frightened and damaged, and if I knew what's good for me, I'd stay out of her life.

I can't offer her more than a roll in the sack, and a few good memories. Not that she's asking for more. She's not. But I need to maintain stability in my life, and stay out of trouble for Cassie's sake. I can't lose her.

"All set?" I ask as she comes toward me, her ponytail bouncing on her shoulders.

A chorus of giggles come from her front door, and I glance up to see her roommates, still dressed in their pajamas and looking like death warmed over. I remember those hangover days. I'm glad they're behind me.

"Morning," I say and give them a wave.

"Morning," they all say. "Are you two *coming* or going?" the dark-haired girl asks. She was the one I'd caught gawking at me the other morning.

"Going," I say, and more giggles sound.

"Oh, too bad," the blonde answers.

I open my mouth to respond, but the whack to the gut stops me.

"Don't encourage them, Jaxon," I say. "Dim-witted moths, remember."

"Right." She starts to walk, and I say, "I can take the car. I might have a lot to carry back."

"Okay." I pull the fob from my back pocket and open the doors. She slides in next to me and that's when I catch her scent. Goddammit, it makes me want to eat her up again. I drive the short distance to the market, park, and meet Rachel at the front of the car.

We make our way to the outdoor market, where we can buy anything from fresh produce and meat to breads, wine, and gifts. I purchase a bottle of wine, and turn to see Rachel looking over the knitted hats and mitts. There is a little girl lost look on her face that tugs at me. I step up behind her, put my mouth near her ear. "Are you getting a new hat?"

She stiffens, and says, "No, it's not that."

I point to the blue hat with the pom poms on the top. "I think that one would look cute on you." I reach for it but her soft voice stops me.

"Mom used to make hats like these for me."

She's not talked about her mom, or her past, so I go still, and wait for her to expand. "She taught me how to knit when I was little," she adds, and I remain quiet, fully aware that she's telling me something important. "I miss it, actually. I just don't have time for it anymore." I put my hand around her, hold her to me, and she leans into me. Her body softens, and she adds, "I miss my mom, too."

I turn her to face me, wanting to ask about her mom, her dad, if she has any siblings, even though I should keep things a little more impersonal. "I'm sorry."

She forces a smile. "It was a long time ago."

"Your dad?" I dare ask.

"He's not...in my life anymore."

My heart pinches. She's as alone in this world as I am. But I have Cassie, and my in-laws. "I don't have any family either," I say. "I was raised in the system. Tossed around and kicked around."

Why the hell am I telling her this?

Her eyes widen. "I'm sorry, Jaxon."

"It's okay. It toughened me up. I was never in prison like your friends said, but I did do a stint in juvie when I was younger." I laugh and add, "I was a fucked up little bastard."

"I think you grew up to be a pretty good guy."

"Oh, yeah. What else do you think?"

"Fishing much?" she says, and we both laugh, as she lightened things up.

"You can tell me later how great I am."

"And big?" she teases.

"Well, yeah, of course." I nudge her. "Right now, let's go get that ice cream?"

We turn and I come face to face with someone I was once very close to.

Jessica's eyes grow wide when she sees me, and not in a happy sort of way. "Jaxon, long time no see." Her steely gaze goes from me to Rachel. "Have you heard from Sarah lately?"

As I look at Sarah's best friend—the girl who stood for us at our wedding—and now blames me for Sarah's drug use, I say, "Can't say as I have."

"Who's this?" she asks and looks Rachel over.

"This is Rachel."

"Freshman?" she asks, the disgust behind her words apparent.

"She's my next door neighbor."

Jessica angles her head, a smirk on her face when she asks, "You two look like you just finished a sex marathon. So, I don't think that's all she is to you."

I clench down hard enough to break bone. "What she is, Jessica, is none of your business."

"Maybe not, but it's definitely Sarah's business, and we both know why."

9

RACHEL

I sit on my bed, my hands on my laptop keyboard, but the words just aren't coming. My mind drifts back to this afternoon, from the conversation about Sarah, to the weird meeting with Jessica at the farm market. I have no idea why she seemed so pleased with herself. And really, is it Sarah's business that I'm with Jaxon? Well, I'm not *with him* with him. I'm just having a brief affair and *she's* the one who's run off with her dealer. Then again, if I'm going to be around her daughter, it does become her business, right? No matter what the circumstances might be, Sarah is still the mother of the child. Jaxon had made that perfectly clear.

It's also perfectly clear that while they might be over, he's never gotten over her. But that's not my burden to bear, really. We both agreed on a brief affair, for our own personal reasons, and neither one of us is looking for anything more.

A bang in the driveway outside reaches my ears. I slip off my bed and walk to my window. A huge floodlight lights up the area between houses and I glance at Jaxon, who's working on my car. Beside him, he has a baby monitor, likely to hear Cassie if she wakes up and needs him. My heart warms at that. Jaxon might be a lot of things, might have had a misguided youth, but he's a great father. I push the window up.

"Can you keep it down, some of us are trying to concentrate."

My legs go weak when he grins at me, and showcases that sexy dimple that makes me want to remove my panties and throw myself at him.

"How's it going anyway?" he asks.

I groan, and glance at my laptop. "It's not."

He wipes his hands with a rag and leans against my car, crossing his ankles. Could the man have picked a sexier pose. God, now I'm never going to get that out of my head.

"What's the problem?" he calls up to me.

"I can't seem to focus." Dammit, when I moved here I swore I was going to keep my head down and concentrate only on school. Why, oh why, did I have to get involved with my neighbor?

Oh, because he's hot and you needed to get laid.

I only hope that after time in his bed, I'll be sexed out, and can refocus on my studies.

"Distracting you, am I?" His sexy grin curls my toes.

I fold my arms and cock my head. "Ego much?"

He laughs, a rich baritone that prowls through my bloodstream and wakes my body. "How about a little incentive?" he asks, a hint of humor in his voice

Dressed in my yoga pants and t-shirt, I lean out a little more. Goosebumps break out on my flesh as I breathe in the cooler night air. "What do you have in mind?"

"How many pages do you have to write?"

"It's a five-hundred-word essay."

"Okay, after every one hundred words, text me to let me know you're done."

I crinkle my nose, having no idea where he's going with this. "How is that incentive?"

He wags his eyebrow. "You'll see."

"I don't know, Jaxon," I say cautiously. What the heck is he up to? I'm not sure, but from the way he's looking at me, I'd hazard a guess that it's sexual. Why does that thrill me so much? Jeez, I'm turning into a regular nymphomaniac, like a few of my roommates.

"Tell me what you're up to first."

"Nope. But if I were you, I'd start writing, because you're going to like it."

"Pretty sure of yourself, aren't you?"

"Yeah," he says, and I laugh.

"It better be good," I say as I close the window.

I hurry back to my bed, and place my phone beside me. I do a quick search on some information that I want to verify, then get to work on the first one hundred words. The sound of Jaxon tinkering outside actually brings me a measure of comfort. I like him close, and that's well...probably not a good thing.

As I listen to him work, I begin my paper, and before I know it, I have the first one hundred words written. I'm on a bit of a roll, and could keep going but I'm too anxious to see what Jaxon is up to.

I'm done, I text.

I wait for his response, my heart pounding as three little ellipses flash on my screen. Then his text comes in, a link to something.

I frown, a bit confused, and slip from the bed and walk to my window. I inch it up and search the driveway. A movement just outside the floodlight catches my attention, and I squint to adjust to the darkness. I make out Jaxon's silhouette in the dark. Why is he hiding in the shadows? I listen, and I'm sure I hear the hiss of his zipper. No freaking way is he doing what

I think he's doing! Yeah, okay, so it totally turned me on when he stroked himself, lacking any sort of modesty as he rubbed his long length while keeping his blue eyes trained on me. I'd never seen a guy do that before. I do a quick search of the street. He's veiled by darkness. No one walking buy would see him, but still what he's doing is risky, inappropriate...exciting.

"Jaxon," I whisper, and glance at the link he'd sent me. I click on it, and nearly bite off my tongue when it takes me directly to a dirty video. "Ohmigod," I say, a little too loudly. When Jaxon's chuckle reaches my ears, I glance over my shoulder to make sure my deadbolt is in place.

I watch the video for a second, take in the guy stroking himself as a naked girl on the bed beckons him. I drag my attention from the screen and search out Jaxon. I hear a grunt, then another and I lean out further.

My phone pings and I glance at the screen.

Like what you see?

I text back. *Yeah, but you're crazy!*

He sends me a laughing emoticon, then texts, *Pause the video, and back to work.*

With my blood racing and my pulse beating wildly at my neck I do as he says and hurry to my bed. As the image of Jaxon masturbating flashes through my mind, I quickly read over my first one-hundred words and get the next few paragraphs down. I grab my phone, and my fingers race over the screen.

Done.

Stay on your bed, put the movie back on and watch it for two minutes.

I read his text, then hit play on the movie. The camera has zeroed in on the naked woman, on her sex to be exact. Her hands slide down her body and she touches herself, spreading her lips wide for her lover. The man drops down, runs his tongue over her, then slides a finger high inside her as she rubs her clit.

Oh. My. God. As I blink, stare, and blink some more, Jaxon's text comes in.

That's what I'm going to do to you when you get your paper done. But that's not all. We're going to reenact the entire scene. Now turn it off, and get the next hundred words done.

Holy Hell!

I resist the urge to touch myself and set the phone beside me, the video on pause. Cripes, I've never watched porn before. I mean, I dipped my toes in once when I clicked on that pop-up link on my laptop, curiosity getting the better of me. But I ended up with a computer virus which crashed my computer, and ended my venture into voyeurism. God, I hope I don't get another virus. Then again, Jaxon wouldn't send me to an infected website. Maybe he has a subscription to the place or something.

I rush to get my next words done, more interested in the video than I ever thought I would be. Then again, maybe it's not so much the video, but the reenactment that's to come later.

Done.

Baby, we're just getting started

That brings a smile to my face.

Now press play and watch for five minutes.

I do as he says, and after the guy finishes tonguing his girl, he slides his cock inside her. My breathing changes, becomes deeper as I watch. I jump from my bed and go to my window. Jaxon is back under the light, his phone in his hand. He glances up when he sees me, then shows me his screen. He's watching the video right along with me. I find that oddly titillating.

The guy fucks the girl on the bed, and pulls out just as my five minutes are up.

Okay, back to work. Get another hundred done, and then you get to watch the next five minutes.

I whip through the next one hundred, even though my thoughts are racing a million miles an hour. I get the words down and grab my phone.

Done.

You're getting faster.

Motivation

He sends me a grinning emoticon, then texts, watch for five more minutes.

With my fingers practically shaking, I hit play. In the video, the guy flips the girl over, and ties her to the bedpost. She's writhing and moaning, and there is a part of me that clenches up. I'm not sure I could ever be restrained like that. Not after surviving an abusive relationship. I'd feel too vulnerable, too out of control. He puts a pillow under her hips, lifting her ass to him, and I audibly gasp, loud enough for Jaxon to hear it.

You okay in there?

I read the text and take in a big breath and let it out slowly. I'm actually touched at the way he's checking in on me. When I don't answer, another text comes in.

I won't tie you up. I won't do anything you don't want. You have to know that by now.

Okay is all I send back.

Finish your last words, and just know what you watch next, yeah, I'm definitely going to that to you. I'm going to claim every inch of you, baby. I'm going to fuck every part of you before this ends between us.

My heart gives one big heavy beat at the reminder of the time line—that this affair comes with an expiration date—but I shake my head to clear it. *This is sex only, Rachel. Sex that you so desperately want...need.*

I pause the video, and type the conclusion to my paper. I

want to get back to Jaxon and the video, but I need to read it over at least once. Something tells me I'm going to be pre-occupied for the rest of the night and won't get a chance. Working hard to keep my focus, I go over the paper, make a few tweaks, then save it. I grin, rather pleased with my work, and the way Jaxon has been motivating me. I grab my phone.

Done

About time. My cock is so fucking hard, I'm ready to blow, but I want to be inside you when I do.

My entire body vibrates, and I'm practically quaking on my bed.

Now watch the video for five more minutes, then get your sweet ass over here.

I'm breathing so hard, I'm sure I'm going to hyperventi-late as I click play. The man on the screen, climbs over the sprawled and tied woman, grabs some lubricant, and inserts a finger into her ass.

"Oh, Jesus," I whisper. Does Jaxon plan to do that to me? I'm not sure if I'm thrilled or terrified by the idea. I stare, shocked as he slowly performs the intimate act, and I'm a hot mess of nerves when he enters her completely. I drop my phone, my panties so damp, I'll have to change before I go to Jaxon's. Then again, maybe I shouldn't. Maybe I should let him know what this all did to me. Deciding to leave my panties on, I bound from the bed, unlock my door and hurry outside. When I reach the driveway, I glance around, but Jaxon is nowhere to be found. The light on his front steps is on, so I hurry to his door.

I lift my hand to knock, but the door swings open. We stand there staring at each other for a moment, then he lifts his hand and presses a finger to his lips.

"Cassie?" I whisper.

"She's asleep. We'll need to be quiet."

After that video and the dirty things this man texted to me, I'm not sure I can be quiet.

"Jaxon," I whisper, about to tell him that when he shifts his stance and goes as still as still as a stealth soldier, his eyes locked on mine. My heart practically stops. I've never seen him so intense before.

"I want you," he says. "I want every inch of you. But before I take you to my room, tell me I can have that, Rach."

I swallow against a tight throat, not sure I can get the words out, so I nod, ready to do almost all of those things on the video.

"Say it," he growls through clenched teeth. "I need to hear you say it."

I have no idea what's come over him, but I have to admit, I like it. "You can have every inch of me," I say.

In a fast move that takes me by surprise, I'm in his arms, and he's carrying me to his room, locking the door behind us. He sets me down, and backs me up until I'm pressed against the wall. His lips come down over mine as he grabs my arms and holds them over my head. He keeps them there with one hand as the other slides down my body, between my breasts.

He pushes his cock against me, letting me know he's as turned on as I am. I move against him, massage his erection with my body. He groans.

"Cut it out, or this will be over before it starts."

"I guess the movie got to you?" I say quietly.

"No, baby," he whispers. "The thoughts of you in my bed tonight is what got to me." He stands back, and his gaze slowly slides the length of me. He scrubs his face, his gaze full of want. "I need you naked. I need to see all of you."

My heart jumps. Honest to God, no man has ever looked at me with such need and hunger before. I reach for the hem of my t-shirt and pull it over my head. Jaxon's eyes latch onto my breasts, my nipples hard and visible though the lace bra. A quake moves through me as he sheds his own t-shirt and reaches for the button on his jeans. He strips quickly, and I take him in. I've never seen a more beautiful man.

"Keep going," he orders in a soft tone. I grip the sides of my yoga pants, give a little extra wiggle to my hips as I shimmy them down my legs. He breathes deeply, and points at my panties. "Give me them."

I slide them down, slowly lift one foot and then the other. He holds one hand out, and I toss them to him. He rubs the material between his thumb and finger. "So nice and wet for me."

"Jaxon," I groan, desperate for his touch.

"Spread your legs, show me that wet pussy."

OMG.

I widen my legs, and he comes close to me, dropping to his knees before me. "Open up babe, let me see."

I reach down and spread my wet lips, and his hot breath washes over my clit as he groans in delight. How is it this man makes me feel so important, like I'm the most beautiful, desirable woman in the world?

He flicks his tongue out to taste me, and my legs go weak as he circles my clit. I moan and reach for him when he goes back on his heels.

"On the bed," he says, and I practically run across the room. His chuckle reaches my ears. I take in his beauty as he comes toward me, his hand on his cock.

"Like what you see?" he asked.

"Yes," I say without hesitation. "This is way better than in the movie you sent me."

"Open your legs, touch yourself for me."

Eager to see his reaction, I slide my hand down to stroke my sopping wet sex.

"Yeah, that's it," he whispers, as he rubs his cock harder. I briefly close my eyes, and tilt my head back as pleasure races through me. "Feel good, Rach?" he asks, his voice so soft, and sweet my eyes open.

"Yes," I murmur, and apply more pressure to my clit.

He drops to his knees by the bed, grips my legs and pulls until their dangling. He shimmies in closer, positioning himself between my legs. "Keep rubbing your hot pussy for me. It's making me so goddamn hard."

I rub and swirl my fingers through my slick heat, his words urging me on and exciting me. "You like that, babe? You like knowing what you do to me?"

"Yes," I say, and slide my finger lower to insert it into my quaking sex.

"Motherfucker," he murmurs, and a half laugh, half moan catches in my throat. "Oh, yeah, you really like fucking with me, don't you?"

"I like fucking you," I say, my bold words surprising me.

Jaxon stands, grips my hips and lifts until my sex is lined up with his. "I like fucking you, too," he says and in one fluid movement, he's high inside me, thrusting hard and deep, filling me so beautifully, I nearly cry out. Stifling my moan, I grip the sheets, and curl them in my fingers as he pumps.

"So good," I murmur.

"Yeah," he agrees. He bends over me, and with his cock still inside me, he shifts us until I'm centered on the bed. He pulls his cock out, and presses his mouth to my sex. He eats at me, and I squirm, my body on hyper drive. One hand slides under my ass, and I stiffen when his fingers rub my puckered opening.

"Jaxon," I murmur. "I never..."

He lifts his head, and his mouth is wet from my juices. "I know," he says quietly. "I'm just going to touch you. If you don't like it, I'll stop."

I nod and relax back into the mattress. His mouth is back on my sex, his tongue lapping at my aching clit as he slowly plays with my back passage. I move against him, and suck in a breath when he slowly presses into me. It's a strange feeling, but I think I might like it. He nibbles my clit and slides lower to push his tongue inside me. My fingers go to my clit, and the triple assault of his finger in my ass, his tongue inside me, and my hands on my clit, push me over the edge. My body lets go, and I come all over his hungry mouth.

"Fuck, Rach," he whispers from between my legs, and stays there lapping at my juices. I moan, writhe on the bed, and race my hands through his hair. When my spasms stop, he climbs up my body and slides his cock back into me.

"God, yes," I say a little too loudly. He presses his mouth to mine to stifle my sounds and I taste myself on his tongue. We kiss, moan, tangle tongues as we fuck. I'm so wet he easily slides in and out, and I lift my hips to welcome each hard thrust. His breathing changes, and he buries his face in my neck.

"Fill me with your cum," I whisper, and he groans as his cock swells inside me, spreading me even more.

I run my hands over his back, revel in his hard muscles as they clench and tighten with each pump. He powers into me, and stills. My eyes roll back as he climaxes. I feel it all, everything from his hot seed filling me to his breath on my neck. Every part of my body is alive, aware of this man's touch, this man's...everything.

He collapses on top of me, and as exhaustion takes over, I close my eyes. I'll just sleep for five seconds, then I'll get dressed and get out of here before morning. The last thing I want is to wake up in his bed, or for his daughter to see me and get the wrong idea.

JAXON

Morning light filters in through the crack in my curtains and wakes me. I stretch, and can't help but smile when I find a sleeping Rachel beside me, breathing softly. I glance at the clock. I still have half an hour before I have to wake my daughter and get her ready for school. Which means, I can wake Rachel first, and do dirty things to her before I take her to school.

I climb over her, and she stirs when I spread her legs and settle the crown of my cock at her sweet opening.

"Jaxon," she murmurs, and her eyes open wide when I slide in an inch. "Oh."

"You awake?" I ask.

"I am now," she says and her head goes from left to right, like she's trying to orient herself. "What time is it?"

"Seven."

Alarm crosses her face. "What about—"

"We have thirty minutes. Enough time for me to fuck you before you have to go."

She opens her mouth like she's about to protest, but when I give her another inch, the words die on her tongue. Her eyes roll and I slide in even more. I power forward to fill her, and seat myself high inside.

"You were saying something," I tease as she clenches around my cock. Dammit, why is sex with her so fucking good?

"I was?"

I chuckle, and close my mouth over hers for a good morning kiss. Her hips move, and I move right along with her. Christ, I could wake up to this every morning. Rachel is quickly becoming an addiction. She slides her hands around me and holds on as I take her.

"If I had my way, I'd tie you to my bedpost and keep you here with me for the day." She stiffens a little, and rage zings through me. I'd love to get my hands on the bastard that hurt her. "Rach—" I begin, ready to remind her that I'd never hurt her or do anything she didn't want but, she presses her finger to my lips to silence me.

"There were a lot of things in that video that we didn't do."

I stop fucking her, and my head goes back. "What are you getting at?"

She draws her bottom lip into her mouth, and I swear to fuck, she never looked sexier. "Maybe I want you to flip me over and fuck me the same way."

Her words shock me. "Jesus, fuck. Rachel. I can't believe..."

"What did you think I meant?" she teases, throwing my words back at me.

"Not that," I say and she laughs. I push her hair from her face, and search her eyes. "Is that something you'd like to try?" I understand it would take a lot of trust on her part to let me do those things to her, and I don't take that lightly.

"I have you for two weeks," she says. "Maybe I'd like to let go once in my life, and...try new things."

I'm not sure what's come over her, but I damn well like it. "Yeah?"

"Yeah," she assures me.

My heart thunders, because there are so many things I want to do with this sweet girl, so many ways I want to claim her.

"And maybe I can do that to you, too," she says.

"What?" I ask, my lust-drunk brain trying to process. "Do what to me?"

"Fuck you like that," she says, her face serious.

I inch back, my cock throbbing inside her. "Wait, what? You want to fuck me in the ass?"

She cocks her head. "What did you think I meant?"

"Not that," I say quickly.

She laughs, her soft chuckle curling around me as I relax back into her. "I'm not serious, Jaxon."

"Thank God."

"But if I was, you'd let me?"

"Only you, Rachel, only you."

Her laugh turns to a moan as I begin to fuck her again. All thoughts leave my brain as my blood rushes south. I slam home, rub my pelvis against her swollen clit, and soon she's coming all over my cock. As her release scorches me, I pound into her, then settle high inside so I can fill her with my cum. It fucks with my mind to know she'll have my cum inside her when she goes to school today, keeping a part of me with her. I like that. Probably a little too fucking much.

"You weren't kidding when you said you were going to make me come every day?" she says, her voice a soft, contented purr.

"You think I'd kid about something like that?" She laughs, and I roll off her. She curls into me and I give her a soft tap on the ass. "We'd bet get a move on. I have to wake Cassie."

She nods, and with slow, relaxed movements that showcase a well-fucked woman, she climbs from the bed. I take in her beautiful body as she searches for her clothes.

She glances at me over her shoulder. "Are you just going to lay there and stare at me?"

"Thinking about it."

"Move," she says, and points a finger at me.

"I'm driving you to school."

"You don't have to. I can walk."

"And I can drive you." She turns, plants one hand on her hip and glares at me. "You're kind of sexy when you're trying to be tough." She stares at me like she doesn't know whether to laugh or smack me. "Makes me want to fuck you all over again." I kick my sheets off, and stalk across the room, my footsteps loud on the floor. I tug her to me, and plant my mouth on hers. She tastes so fucking good, I'm not sure we'll ever get out of this room, but the jiggling of my door knob stops me.

"Daddy?"

"Oh shit," I mutter. Rachel backs up, and I scan the floor for my clothes. I grab my pants, and Rachel tosses me my T-shirt. I hurry into them.

"I don't want her to get the wrong idea, Jaxon," Rachel says quietly, her lashes blinking rapidly.

I scrub my face, and think about this turn of events. Fuck, I need to be more careful where Cassie is concerned. She's my one priority in life, and I don't want to fuck her up. She's been through enough already. "I know."

Rachel hurries to the bed, and starts to make it, and that's when I clue in to what she's doing. She's as smart as she is beautiful. I open the door to find a sleepy Cassie rubbing her eyes. "Why are you up?" I ask her.

"I heard noises." Her eyes open wide when she looks across the room. "Rachel!" she says, and my heart misses a beat. Apparently, I'm not the only one who likes our neighbor.

"Good morning, Cassie." she says as she tucks the blankets in.

"Why are you here?"

"I'm here to help around the house, remember?"

Her nose crinkles as she thinks about that. "Will you help me with my bed?"

I open my mouth to tell her she can make her own bed, but Rachel reaches for her hand and says, "Sure."

"I'll start breakfast," I say as my daughter drags our neighbor across the hall. I make a quick trip to the bathroom, then head to the kitchen. First thing I need is coffee. I'm sure Rachel does too. After I get the coffee going, I grab some eggs and start on an omelet. I'm almost done before I hear my girls coming down the hallway.

My girls.

Shit.

"Hey what took you so long?" I ask, but when I turn to see Cassie's dressed, with a freshly scrubbed face, and braids, I realize how helpful Rachel is with my daughter.

"Look, Daddy," Cassie says and does a twirl. "Rachel does a perfect twisted pony."

"I see," I say as she hops into her chair. I pour her orange juice as Rachel grabs two mugs and gets our coffee ready like she's done this a million times before. Our hands brush as I take the mug from her, and I swear to fuck the electricity that just arced between us was enough to set my house on fire.

"Daddy, I don't want to go to school today."

My head rears back, concern tightening my gut. "But you love school."

She frowns, and narrows her eyes. "When I'm on the swings, Jacob keeps pulling my hair."

"Have you told your playground monitor?"

"She says boys do that when they like girls. That's stupid, Daddy."

A sound catches in Rachel's throat and all eyes turn to her. She's shaking her head as she pulls a chair out from the table and sinks into it. "Cassie, honey, no one should ever touch you when you don't want to be touched."

"I told him to stop and he wouldn't." She forks a big piece of omelet into her mouth.

Rachel nods. "I understand. I'm glad you told him to stop. Using your words is good."

"But he won't stop, and everyone laughs."

"If it happens again, can you go to your teacher?" Rachel asks gently.

A smile lights up Cassie's face. "I like Miss Tammy."

Rachel pats my daughter's hand. "Good, I bet she'll put a stop to it."

Rachel stands to refill her coffee, and she has a stricken look on her face. Cassie grabs her kids iPad and turns it on, and we move out of earshot.

I take her mug and pour her another cup, and our eyes meet.

"It's not cute and it's not sweet for any boy to be rough with her," Rachel begins. "I can't believe her playground monitor said that. It's not an acceptable sign of affection, Jaxon."

I shake my head. "Playground bullies. I've had my share."

She frowns and puts her hand on my cheek. "What did you do?"

"I learned to fight, real fast. Good thing too. I never would have survived juvie if I hadn't learned how to defend myself early in life."

"I'm sorry you had to go through that."

I shrug. "It's the past. I'm worried about Cassie. It's different for girls."

"Very," she says. "Condoning or justifying behavior at this age, teaching girls it's okay to be mistreated leads to women staying in abusive relations." She swallows hard and turns from me, but I stop her and drag her back.

"Rach," I say, and put a hand on her shoulder, only to find her trembling. "Are you okay?"

"Yeah, I'm...it's harmful to teach little girls that it's okay to be mistreated."

"You're right."

"My mom taught me that at a very young age. Maybe because she was in her own bad relationship and couldn't get out. She didn't want to see that happen to me." She lets out a humorless laugh. "In the end I didn't fall far..."

Her words die on her lips, and as Cassie munches away on her breakfast, I pull Rachel to me. "You got out, Rach. You're safe now. I'm not going to let anything happen to you."

She nods, but there is worry, skepticism in her eyes when she pulls away.

"You and your mom were close?" I ask, wanting to know so much more about this beautiful woman.

She nods, plasters on a smile, and says, "I'd better get ready. I don't want to make Cassie late for school."

She hands me her cup. "You're not staying for breakfast?"

"I'll grab a muffin."

I nod. "Do you work tonight?"

"No, night off, thank God."

"Have dinner with us."

"Daddy, are we having spaghetti," Cassie calls out and I freeze. Jesus, I hope she hadn't overheard anything we were saying.

"Probably," I say.

"How about I make that salmon you picked up at the

market." Before I can answer, Rachel turns to Cassie and calls out, "Do you like salmon, Cassie?"

"No, but Daddy makes me eat it."

Rachel laughs. "I bet you'll like it the way I make it."

"Probably not," Cassie says and we both laugh. I give Rachel a tap on the ass to get her moving. "You've got forty-five minutes, and don't think about walking. If you do, you'll be sorry."

"Oh, really?" she asks, a bit of intrigue in her eyes.

"Yeah, I'll stop the car, put you over my shoulder and toss you into the back seat."

"You wouldn't."

"You want to try me?"

"Ah, no."

"Good, now go."

I walk her to the door, and when I'm certain Cassie isn't looking, I give her a quick kiss.

"I probably shouldn't stay over anymore. That was risky this morning."

"Yeah, I know."

"You're going to have to stop making me too weak to move."

I grin at her. "I'll do my best."

"I know, you always do your best and that's why I can't move my legs."

She gives me that weird little finger waves that rocks my cock and bolts down the stairs. I watch her sweet ass in those tight yoga pants until she's out of sight, then head back to the kitchen to get Cassie's lunch packs. Since Rachel got her dressed and her hair done, the morning is going to go that much smoother.

I toss Cassie's plate in the sink, gulp back my breakfast, and prepare her lunch. Since we have a few minutes to spare, I let her go play on the swings in the back yard while I tinker with Rachel's car and wait for her to appear.

I totally forgot to tell her that I found a radiator core for a good price from my buddy's junk yard. If it gets here quick enough, I should be able to have her car ready sooner rather than later. That though hits like a punch to the gut. Once I'm done, she'll no longer be in my house, my bed. Dammit, maybe I should draw this vehicle repair out a little longer. At least until Thanksgiving. I mean, she said she was a great cook, and Cassie and I sure could use a decent meal on Thanksgiving.

Shit, how is that for illogical thinking at its worst?

Just then my phone vibrates and I pull it from my pocket. Since I fully expect it to be Rachel texting me, a little jolt of excitement pulses through my veins. Except when I see who's calling, my heart crashes against my ribcage.

"Everything okay?"

Rachel's voice pulls my focus and I slide the phone back into my pocket. "Yeah, fine."

She angles her head, her eye moving over me. "Are you sure? You look like you've seen a ghost."

Cassie comes running toward us, and that saves me from having to answer. "All set, kiddo," I say, and open the back door for her. "I'll be right back. I just have to grab her backpack and lunch."

I hurry through the house, unease racing through me as I pull my phone from my back pocket and look at Sarah's message. *Hey jay.*

Jay, that was her nickname for me. She used to use it when she was being playful, or wanted something from me.

After all this time, why was she reaching out now and what the fuck does she want from me? I stare at the phone for a moment and debate on asking that question, but I have Cassie and Rachel to take care of and don't have time for this right now. I grab Cassie's backpack and lunch and rush back outside.

"All set?" I ask as I tug on my belt.

"You sure you're okay?" Rachel asks, and I avoid her questioning eyes as I back from the driveway.

"Listen, I meant to tell you, I found a radiator core for a good price."

"Really, that's great. What about the rod thingy you were talking about?"

I grin at her. "Look at you, talking shop with me." I wink and say. "Tie rod end and I'm looking into that now."

"Do you think you'll be able to get a deal?"

"Probably."

"Then the car will be done soon?" I glance at her and can't tell whether that's happiness or disappointment on her face. Sure, she wants her car back, but is she ready for this thing to be over between us. I probably shouldn't be so concerned about that.

"Yeah, but I'll have to do a wheel alignment after I repair it."

"So I'm guessing at least another week."

Not really.

"Yeah, something like that." I reach Cassie's school and pull up to the curve. She unbuckles as I slide from my seat. Before she can take off, I bend and say, "Now you remember what to do if Jacob pulls your hair, right?"

"I remember, Daddy."

"Okay, good girl." I give her a kiss on the forehead and says, "Now go have a good day."

She skips off, and I give the playground monitor a wave as she ushers Cassie into the schoolyard.

"You're a good dad," Rachel says when I buckle back in.

"I'd do anything in the world for her."

"I know." I give her a quick glance. "That was a good cover this morning."

"We need to be careful that never happens again."

I frown. The last thing I need is for Cassie to attach herself to Rachel, or look at her as a mother figure. As I think of her biological mother, my mind races back to Sarah's text and I swallow against a tightening throat. I want her to be a part of Cassie's life, but only if she's clean, and has no plans to run off again. No fucking way will I let her hurt our daughter.

"Agreed," I say. "It can never happen again." Without thinking my hands slides across the seat and captures hers. I run my thumb over her cold hands. "I miss the heat wave already."

"So do my roommates," she says and I can tell by her grin that she's lightening my mood.

I shake my head. "You need to get out of that house."

She laughs. "I guess they're really not that bad. Sylvie told me she had a French maid outfit I could wear for when I'm cleaning your place."

Oh, maybe I like these girls more than I thought.

She leans back, a tiny, mischievous smile on her face. What is going through that brilliant mind of hers?

"You know you can't do that, right?" I say.

She angles her head, and blinks at me. "Do what?"

"Wear a French maid costume around me."

"Oh," she says.

"What did you think I meant?" I ask as I take the turn to her campus.

"That. That you didn't like French Maid costumes."

I squeeze her hand. "Believe me, Rach. I'd love it on you but if you ever came near me in one, I'd blow before I ever got inside you, and you know how much I like filling you with my cum."

She squeezes her legs, and memories of this morning jump

to the forefront of my brain. I put my hand on her thigh, and she exhales a slow breath, the sound reminding me of air being let go from a balloon. Her cheeks turn a pretty shade of pink, and I have to say, I like when she gets all sexually flustered.

"I'm probably going to have to pay you back for this," she says as I pull up to the curb.

"Back for what?" I ask, feigning innocence.

She glares at me. "How do you expect me to concentrate when you say things like that to me?"

"If you can't concentrate, we could always try that video technique that got you back on track last night."

"Oh, yeah, I'm definitely going to pay you back for this." She whacks my chest and I laugh.

"Well, for what it's worth, I'm probably going to have to go home and tug one out," I say bluntly, just to get a reaction out of her.

"Ohmigod, Jaxon," she says and reaches for the door handle like she's in need of a quick escape.

I capture her arm. "Wait." She turns to me, and I settle my lips over hers. She tastes like coffee and mint. I kiss her a little longer, not quite ready for her to go just yet. When our lips break apart, we're both breathless. "What time do your classes finish?"

"Three, but I can walk."

"And I can pick you up."

"Jax—"

I point downward. "I'll be right here, at three."

She rolls her eyes at me and exits the vehicle. She does a quick scan of the area, like she always does, and then catches up with friends. She angles her head to see I'm still watching, and when she finds me still here, she gives me that awkward wave that always thickens my dick. Yeah, I'm definitely going to have to rub one out.

Chuckling to myself, I head back home, and after a quick shower, I get to work on the cars in my shop. Time slips by, my morning gone before I realize it. I grab a sandwich. As I eat, I wonder what Rachel is doing for lunch. Something tells me she skips a lot of meals. I make a mental note to make a lunch for her when I'm making Cassie's.

I head back downstairs and my buddy Jericho pulls up to the curb. "What's up?" I say as he walks toward me.

"Do you have time for a safety inspection?" he asks as he adjusts the ball cap on his head.

I close the hood on Rachel's car. "Yeah, sure," I say but from the way he's looking at me I'm guessing he has something on his mind. I'm about to ask him what's up when my phone rings.

My heart lurches when I see its Cassie's school calling. "Shit. I have to take this?" I slide my finger across the phone and pace the length of the driveway as the principal alerts me to an incident on the playground.

"I'll be right there," I say. Fuck, man, I spent more time in the principal's office than I can recount. I never in this lifetime expected to get a call about Cassie, though. Shit, if the in-laws get a whiff of this...Nothing good could come from it. Nothing good at all.

I end the call and turn to find a very concerned friend eyeing me. "I have to go."

"Everything okay?" he asks, like he knew who the caller was.

"Cassie punched a guy in the face at school. That was the principal."

Jericho cringes, clearly not expecting that from me. I want to ask what he knows, why he just showed up out of the blue, but I have other more important things on my mind right now.

"Jesus," he says, and shoves his keys into his pocket. "Want me to come with you?"

"No, I got this." It's a lie. I don't got this. I'm so overprotective of my daughter, I fear I'll do or say the wrong thing. I breathe and think of Cassie, and what's best for her. She might need someone with a softer touch today, someone with clear reasoning skills. Unfortunately, I'm worried that someone is not me.

"Okay, call me if you need me," Jericho says, and climbs back into his car. I watch him disappear around the corner, out of sight, and before I can think better of it I shoot a text off to Rachel.

Hey, do you have any free time?

I wait a moment and her text comes in. *What's up? Just headed to lecture hall.*

Cassie punched Jacob in the face. The school just called. I'm headed there now. I just...not sure how to handle this. Any advice?

I'll go with you.

I feel a measure of relief. But the truth is, I shouldn't be relying on Rachel like this, or pulling her away from her classes.

What about class? I text.

The lectures are recorded. I'll watch it tonight.

I let loose a slow breath. *Thanks Rach.*

I end the call, shove my phone into my pocket and lock the house. I drive quickly to her campus and find her standing at the spot I'd dropped her off at a few hours earlier. My heart leaps, a little too happy that she's helping me out with this. She hurries into the car, and her eyes are wide when they meet mine.

"What happened?"

"I don't know, really. All I was told was that Cassie punched Jacob during lunch on the playground."

She goes quiet for a second, like she's searching the recesses of her mind. "Oh no."

"What?"

"What if she overheard us this morning. You were talking about how you handled playground bullies, remember?"

"Yeah, but she was playing music." I think about that. "Still...I guess maybe she did hear." I run my fingers through my hair. "Fuck, if she tells the principal that, I'm sure child protection services will be called in."

"Oh, God, Jaxon. That won't be good, but I was there, and witnessed the whole thing. I will assure them you never told your daughter to do such a thing."

I nod, and slide my hand across the seat to grab hers, hold her much like I did this morning on the way to school. It's amazing how life can change in a heartbeat. It's something I should be used to by now, I guess. Sarah left ours in an instant, and Rachel entered it.

"Everything will be okay," Rachel says, and puts her other hand over mind, giving it a gentle squeeze.

"I'm sorry for dragging—"

"Stop. I'm here to help you with anything while you fix my car, and that includes you daughter."

"Okay, thanks."

We both go quiet as I take the corner leading to Cassie's school. I park and take in a breath as I meet Rachel on the sidewalk. I hurry ahead, and Rachel practically jogs along with me. Inside, we head to the principal's office.

"Want me to wait out here?" Rachel ask.

"No, come in."

We both enter, and find Cassie sitting on a chair in front of the secretary's desk. "Daddy," she says and comes running to me. My heart lurches when I see that she's been crying. In another chair along the wall I spot a boy, who has ice on his cheek. I can only assume he's Jacob. His parents must not be here yet.

Principal Emily Hawkins comes from her office. "Mr. Morgan, Cassie…" she hesitates when she sees Rachel. "Will you all come this way please."

We step into her office. "Mr. Hawkins, this is Rachel…" I pause for a second, because it suddenly occurs to me that I don't know Rachel's last name.

Rachel sticks her hand out. "Nice to meet you," she says without offering up her last name either. That bothers me more than I would like. "I'm the next-door neighbor, and babysitter."

"Very well then please have a seat." As we all sit, Cassie settles on my lap, looking sullen and frightened. Mrs. Hawkins continues. "As I said on the phone, Cassie punched Jacob in the face today. We don't tolerate any sort of violence in this school."

"He pulled my hair again, Daddy. It hurts."

"I know," I say to her, and give her a little hug. I glance at Mrs. Hawkins. "Cassie didn't want to come to school today. Jacob has been pulling her hair."

"She mentioned that, but a punch to the face is pretty severe retaliation, and worth an investigation, don't you think. I mean, after all, girls like Cassie…"

"What's that supposed to mean?" I ask, instantly going on the defense.

The principal sits up a little straighter. "Well, Cassie doesn't have any female influences in her life. Perhaps she's learning the wrong things at home."

"If you think—"

Rachel's hand on my arm stops me. "She does have female influences. She has her grandmother and she has me, and you can be rest assured that none of us, including Jaxon, would teach her to do such a thing. What the real issue here is, why has Jacob been allowed to pull her hair, even after she reported it to the playground monitor?"

I take in Rachel's calm demeanor, and try to get myself under control.

"I don't condone violence of any sorts, but as far as I'm concerned, Cassie was defending herself," Rachel continues. "Not in the way we would have preferred, but the boy in the chair out there..." She pauses and point to the window separating the principal's office from the secretary's, "...has been mistreating her. Yet nothing was done until she fought back. Do you know what that does, Mrs. Hawkins?" Rachel doesn't wait for her to respond. "That creates a 'boys will be boys' culture, and teaches girls that unwanted touches are acceptable. Except that hair pulling eventually turns into a tug on the elbow, or other things I'd rather not discuss in Cassie's presence."

"I don't necessarily think it turns into—"

"Maybe not in every case, but definitely in too many. Why wouldn't it, when society makes excuses for such behavior? If you're calling Jaxon's parenting into question here, rest assured, he's one of the best fathers I know, and I'd be more than happy to tell child protection services that."

A noise sounds on the other side of the glass pane, and I turn to see the little boy's mother.

"Well, I don't think that's necessary," Mrs. Hawkins says, and makes a note in her file.

"We'll talk to Cassie about the incident, and we expect she won't be coming home telling us about Jacob touching her again."

Rachel stands, and I stand right along with her. I stare at her, seeing a whole different side to the quiet girl next door, one who is in hiding from someone who did some horrible things to her, clearly. My blood boils, wanting nothing more than to hunt the bastard down and hurt him, but I work to keep my composure for everyone's sake.

I hold Cassie to me, and Jacob's mother keeps her head down in a nervous, intimidated way that has me worried that Jacob's learned behavior comes from home. Cassie remains quiet as I buckle her in, and I let loose a breath before I climb into the driver's seat.

I start the car and turn to find Rachel staring at me. "What you did in there...thank you. You're going to make one hell of a lawyer, Rach."

Her smile is soft and slow. "Thank you. Now let's get her home so we can have a talk with her."

Home.

Odd how both Rachel and I think of my place as home. She's been spending a lot of time there but... I cut my thoughts off, not like the direction they're going.

"Daddy, am I in trouble?"

"No, you're not. But we'll have a little talk when we get home. First we're going to get ice cream, though."

"Daddy?"

"Yeah, kiddo."

"I don't think Jacob will pull my hair anymore."

I stifle a laugh, and Rachel bites her bottom lip beside me. "I don't think he will either."

RACHEL

Rachel

Thankful that's it's Friday, I tug my coat tighter around my waist and exit the campus. My gaze goes straight to the spot Jaxon has been dropping me off and picking me up at every day for the last week. I smile the second I see him, and hurry toward his car. It's insane how I've gotten so used to him doing things for me as we engage in a secret affair. Never in my life have I relied on anyone, well, after my mom died, that is. We actually relied on each other, and there isn't a day that I don't miss her. Since I lost her, I've had no choice but to be independent, and self-sufficient, and if I'm not careful, when this thing between us is over, it could very well have an emotional impact. The truth is, over the last couple weeks, I've gotten a little too close to this family, closer than I would have liked.

"How was your day?" he asks as I slide into the passenger seat.

"Not bad. How about you?"

"Good," he says and after I buckle up he pulls into traffic.

I turn and glance at Cassie, who's holding a bright pink card. "Hey, Cassie. What's that you have there?"

"Gina's having a birthday party." She holds the invitation out for me to see, and kicks her legs out with excitement.

"Oooh, that will be fun. Is Gina turning six?"

Cassie nods, and the ponytail I put in her hair earlier this morning after sneaking out of Jaxon's room before the alarm went off, bounces with her glee. "She's older than me."

"Not by much, you'll be six in a couple of months," Jaxon says.

Her big blue eyes go wide. "Can I have a party too, Daddy?"

"Of course." Jaxon looks at me. "We need to go pick up a gift. I'll drop you off at home, then take Cassie to the mall. She's going to her grandparents for supper, and overnight. I took some steaks out for us. I thought I'd barbecue when I got back."

I smile at that. I've been enjoying the meals we've all been sharing, maybe a little too much, and I'm kind of putting on weight. "Actually, I could come with you," I say casually. "I work the late shift so I have plenty of time. Besides, I need to pick up a pair of mittens." I hold up my bare hands. "I seem to have lost mine." Truthfully when I left New York, there were plenty of things I left behind in my hurry to leave my ex in the rearview mirror. "It's getting cold fast."

He scrubs his hands though his hair, and I study his face. Ever since Cassie found me in his room that morning, he's been acting a bit 'off', distracted. But maybe it has more to do with the incident at the principal's office. He's scared of losing his daughter, but if I have anything to do with it, it won't ever happen.

"You sure?" he asks.

"Positive."

I set my backpack on the floor, and settle in for the trip to the mall. Jaxon pulls into a spot near the main entrance. We all climb from the car and Jaxon reaches for Cassie's hand. My heart jumps a little when she grabs mine too and squeals, "Swing me."

Jaxon looks at me, his eyes questioning. I nod and we both lift her into the air as we hurry across the parking lot. When we reach the front doors the small hairs on the back of my neck stand up straight, and I go still.

"More, more," Cassie cries out as Jaxon gives me a concerned look.

"What is it?" he asks, and looks past my shoulder.

"I just got a chill," I say, and try to brush off my unease. "I really do need those mittens." Jaxon stares at me for a moment longer, and when he finally drops it and opens the door for us, I'm grateful. I really don't want to drag my demons into the open, or let them interfere with the last few days I have with Jaxon.

"So what do you think we should get for Gina?" I ask, as I lead her to the big toy store.

"A Barbie doll," she says excitedly. "That's what I want for my birthday."

"Okay, easy enough," I say. We hit the store, and since Cassie knows exactly where the dolls are she grabs my hand and practically drags me through the aisles. We reach the toy section and she squeals. The hollowed-out part of my soul weeps when I see the dolls, the sight taking me back to my childhood with my mom. Every little girl needs a mom, and it breaks my heart that Cassie doesn't have one. I told the principal I was a positive influence in her life, and dammit, as long as I live next door, that's exactly what I plan to do—even after the car is done. There is no reason we can't remain friends.

From behind, Jaxon puts his mouth near my ear. "You okay?"

"Yeah."

"You want one too?" he teases as we stare at the dolls.

I sniff, and laugh. "It's not my birthday."

"When is your birthday?"

I don't normally give too much information about after I fled New York, but find myself saying, "Tenth of December. When's yours?"

"Summer baby. Ninth of June."

"What do you want for your birthday?" he asks quietly as Cassie examines all the dolls and chats endlessly to herself.

Stability. Never have to run again. A happy life. A family of my own—one just like Jaxon's. I nearly swallow my tongue at that last unexpected thought. Since I don't see any of those things in my future, I say, "I don't need anything."

"I never asked you want you needed. I asked you want you wanted." He turns me, and lifts my chin until we're eye to eye. I instantly see want shimmering in the depths of his gorgeous blue eyes and my body reacts.

"Daddy, let's get this one," Cassie says, breaking the intimate moment. I step back to examine the doll.

"I think it's perfect."

"Me, too," Jaxon agrees, but when his eyes meet mine I get the sense that our conversation is not over. We walk to the cash register, pay for the doll, and head into one of the less expensive department stores so I can grab a pair of mittens, and a new hat.

"They're not nearly as nice as the ones at the market," Jaxon says.

"They were nice, weren't they?" I say, not bothering to tell him I need all my pennies for the important things like food, school, and a roof over my head. I'm buried in student loans, and need to be very careful.

Cassie looks up at me with those big blue eyes. "I like this hat, Rachel," she says and it warms my heart. She might have wealthy in-laws, but her father is definitely teaching her money isn't everything.

Jaxon checks his watch. "We'd better get going. Your Grandma and Grandpa are going to be at the house any minute and we still need to get you packed."

"Yay," she says and when we leave the mall we're once again swinging her until we get to the car. Jaxon takes us back to his place, and we all climb from the car. The music in my house is the first thing that reaches my ears. Another Friday, another party. Ugh, how will I make it to spring? I'm not sure, but I'm going to have to start the search for a new place then. I don't think I can do another year with all the partying. Then again, maybe they'll get it out of their system, and straighten up next year.

"Guess you're sleeping at my place tonight," Jaxon whispers in my ear as we head inside.

"Oh, you think?"

"Yeah, I think. Music or no music, that was the plan all along."

I laugh. "Pretty sure of yourself."

"We got the place to ourselves, Rach, and I'm going to make your moans drown out the music next door."

My heart leaps, and a little idea forms in the back of my mind. "Maybe I'll do that to you, instead."

He grins, unlocks the door, and ushers us all inside just as the in-laws pull up to the curve.

"Grandma and Grandpa are here," Cassie yells. "I need to pack."

"Come on, I'll help you," I say quickly, not wanting to be left alone with them. The conversation was awkward and stifled last time. No way do I want to go through that again.

I capture Cassie's hand and she skips as we head down the hall. I grab her overnight bag, and sit on her bed. I love what Jaxon did with her room. All pretty and pink, with rainbows painted on the wall. Then again, perhaps it was Cassie's mother who'd done it before she left. My gaze goes to the picture on her nightstand. Mother and daughter, and my heart aches, thinking about my own ruined frame and picture. I didn't have a lot of time or room to take all the things I wanted, but no way was I fleeing without that picture of Mom and me.

I examine the picture as Cassie pulls clothes from her dresser. She's chatting about what she wants to do for her birthday party, and I'm half listening as I touch the frame. Cassie looks like she's about three in the photo. My gaze roams to her mom. She's breathtaking, and I can totally see the resemblance of mom and daughter, and definitely understand why Jaxon is still in love with her. A pang of sadness settles in my stomach.

Easy, Rach. This is a sex only affair with a timeline.

"That's Mommy," Cassie says flatly, and I lift my head to see her staring at me.

"She's very pretty, Cassie. Like you." I set the photo back down and listen to the voices down the hall as Jaxon speaks with his in-laws.

"Grandma and Grampa told me Mommy loves me."

I hold my arms out to Cassie and she comes to me. I give her a hug, and pull the elastic from her hair. "I'm sure she loves you very much." Cassie shrugs and I reach for the brush on her nightstand. As I run it through her long, blonde curls, Cassie frowns at the picture.

"Daddy wants me to keep this on my nightstand. He doesn't want me to forget Mommy."

"Mommies are very special."

She goes quiet, and I wonder what's going through that busy brain of hers. "Do you have a mommy?"

"Not anymore."

"Do you miss her?"

"Very much." Needing a chance in subject, I say, "I bet Gina is going to love her doll."

"She's going to love it."

"Do you want your hair in a ponytail, or do you want to leave it down?"

"Down," she says and bounds away, bouncing back from mommy conversation much quicker than me. I help her put all her clothes into her bag and follow her to the bathroom to get her toothbrush. Jaxon's voice has lowered significantly as he speaks to his in-laws in the front entrance way.

Once ready, she runs down the hall and throws her arms around her grandmother and it brings a smile to my face. Judy lifts her head, and her smile falters a bit when she sees me. "Nice to see you again, Rachel," she says.

"You as well," I say, and smile at both her and Karl. I turn to Jaxon, who blinks quickly when he catches me studying him. I'm not sure what they were talking about, but it must have been serious, judging from the concerned look on his face.

"She has a party to go to at two tomorrow," Jaxon informs them. "If you could have her back here at one."

"We'll drop her off at the party. Just let us know where."

"You sure?"

"We want all the time we can get with her," Karl says and picks up her bag. Jaxon produces the invitation. "The address is on here. I'll pick her up at four when it's over."

"Perfect." Karl bends to his granddaughter. "How about pizza tonight?"

"Yay, I love pizza."

Jaxon gives his daughter a kiss and hug before her grand-parents lead her out the door. Once gone, Jaxon locks up and turns to me.

"About those steaks."

"Everything okay?" I ask and follow him into the kitchen.

"Yeah, sure."

Between my father and my ex, I can easily tell when

someone is lying or keeping things from me. It's not my business, but Jaxon is clearly upset and I don't like seeing him like this.

"Jaxon, what is it you're not telling me?"

He lowers himself onto a kitchen chair and pulls me onto his lap. He takes a big breath, lets it out slowly and says, "I got a text from Sarah last week."

"Really?"

"Yeah, came out of nowhere."

"Why now?"

"If I had to guess, I'd say it had to do with our run-in with Jessica. They were best friends and maybe they're still in contact."

I stiffen in his arms. A text from Sara. Is that what had him distracted for the last week? Here I thought it had to do with either Cassie nearly catching us in bed together, or the incident at the school, but maybe I was wrong. Maybe the thoughts of seeing Sara again has him preoccupied. Why wouldn't it? He still loves her and wants her to come back to them clean.

"Oh. What did she want?" I ask, not sure if I really want to hear the answer.

"Not sure. Judy heard from her too out of the blue. She's said she thinks she might have been able to talk her in to coming home."

"Oh, wow."

"That could just be hopeful thinking, though. I didn't want to burst her bubble or anything, but Sarah's has a knack for saying what you want to hear. So many times she told me she was going to get clean. She convinced me every one of those times. I guess I just wanted to believe it, you know. There was a child involved."

I nod as I think about that. "How did you two meet? You guys don't seem..." I let my words fall off and Jaxon laughs.

"Don't know how to say, I'm from the wrong side of the tracks, delicately?"

I crinkle my nose, and hope I hadn't hurt his feelings. "Sorry."

"Don't be. I was, and I hung out at a bar. It's now called Jericho's after my buddy bought it. It's not in a great neighborhood. Jericho and I go way back. He's a good guy. Married to a great girl. You'd like her. I should introduce you guys," he says like it's an afterthought, but I can't imagine why he would do that. We're not in a real relationship here.

I nod, and he continues. "Anyway, one night this beautiful blonde walks in with two of her girlfriends." He rolls one shoulder. "It was easy to tell they were rich college girls, and we knew what they wanted."

"What?"

"Bored little rich girls looking for a hit, and a quick fuck with a bad boy." I cringe. "Sorry, I don't mean to be crude, but that's the best way to explain it."

"So you gave her what she wanted?"

"By the time I met her, I was getting my shit together. I'd finished community college, thanks to Jericho's help, and had just become a licensed mechanic. But yeah, basically I gave her what she wanted."

"And you fell in love."

He shakes his head and blows out a breath. "Did we ever." I go quiet, wait for him to continue. He finally breaks the silence and says, "I set up shop here, and she was still living at home and going to school. We spent all our spare time together, but her parents hated me. Sometimes I wonder if Sarah made her choices just to piss them off." He scrubs his chin. "But the drugs, she was getting in deeper, and she started failing classes. She eventually quit and moved in with me. I tried to help her and we went to addiction counseling together."

"I know a lot about addiction. My dad was a mean alcoholic."

His arms tighten around me. "I'm sorry."

"Thanks. Go on," I say, not wanting to talk about me.

"When she got pregnant, she got clean. Everything was perfect and we were so happy. God, we were happy, Rach. Even her parents had softened to me. Life was perfect."

"And then..."

"And then Cassie was born, and I don't know if it was post-partum, but she started sneaking around, doing drugs behind my back when I was working." He swallows, hard. "Jesus fuck, Rach. She was doing drugs while she was taking care of our daughter. I couldn't have that." He tugs on his hair. "I just couldn't. We started to fight, and things just escalated from there. None of this was good for Cassie. I grew up in volatile homes and I swore I'd do better for my child."

I brush my hand through his hair and press my lips to his forehead. He holds me tighter, and no matter how many times we've been naked together, he's been inside me, I've never felt closer to him. I hug him and his heart pounds against my chest.

"One night while we were sleeping, she left. I found out later she left with her dealer. Her parents don't know the extent of her drug use, they just think I drove her away."

"I bet on some level they know better. It's just hard for them to admit their daughter might be responsible for everything that's happened. I'm sure it's hard for them to think Sarah walked out on her small child."

"You're probably right."

"Parents always side with their child," I say, thinking about my grandmother. "What will you do if she comes back?"

He goes quiet, too quiet, and looks down at my lap. "I

guess it's going to depend on what kind of state she's in." His head lifts, a sadness in his eyes. "Rach?"

"Yeah."

"I don't really talk about this."

"I know." Clearly, she gutted him, broke this amazing man's life into pieces that he's not yet been able to put back together. If she comes back, will it right his life again? Where does that leave me?

Oh, God, Rachel, you can't let yourself fall for this man...this family. They're not yours.

JAXON

I zip up my leather jacket as I walk the few blocks to Pizza Villa. Rach isn't expecting me, but I can't wait one more second to see her. After our steaks, she packed a bag for my place for the night and headed to work. Then again, she probably didn't need a bag. More and more of her laundry was landing in my basket, and it's weird how much I like that.

A car passes slowly, and once it rounds the corner I go still to search the shadows. A strange sensation that someone is watching me, has the hairs on my nape rising. What the fuck? When my search comes up empty, I shake my head. Jesus, maybe I've been hanging around Rachel too much. She's always watching her back and checking the streets.

I brush it off, tug open the door to the pizza joint, and the scent of pepperoni hits me, but it's not pizza I'm hungry for. I'm not sure why I can't get enough of the girl next door—my daughter's babysitter—and her car is basically done, minus the alignment. I could have that finished in a heartbeat for her, but I've been putting it off.

There are two frat guys at the counter, and Rachel is

serving them. They're loud and obnoxious and have obviously been drinking. I stand there for a moment, and admire the way she handles them. They pay and step back. Her eyes lift to serve me and the smile that crosses her face just about fucks me over.

I'm crazy about her.

"Hey," she says. "What are you doing here?" She laughs and adds, "What a stupid question. What can I get for you?"

I need a quick second to pull myself together after that epiphany. "How about your number?" I tease.

She angles her head, and gives me a coy look. "Why should I do that?" she asks, playing along.

"So I can call you?"

"What would you want to call me for?"

"To make plans?"

"What kind of plans."

I lean across the counter, and whisper, "To get you in my bed."

Heat moves into her cheeks and she does a quick check over her shoulder to make sure no one heard me. "I get off in ten minutes," she says, sounding far more breathless.

"You'll get off when I get you into my bed," I say with a grin.

She blows her hair from her face. "Ohmigod, Jaxon, you're going to get me fired."

"I wanted to talk to you about that anyway," I say without thinking it through.

What the hell are you doing, dude.

"Yeah?"

I step back. "Finish up. I'll wait here for you."

"You want me to make a pie for us?"

"No, we're going out," I say, an instant decision. She'd been busy studying and working and taking care of us all week. She needs a break.

Her eyes widen, but she pulls herself together when a co-worker comes from the back to take over the cash. She disappears out back, and I grab a table, my thoughts a million miles an hour. Fuck. I like her, too much, and by rights I should just finish her car and end it. I have a shit-ton going on in my life, Sarah might be coming home, and Rach could up and run at a moment's notice, or at least decide we weren't enough for her.

Wait, what exactly do you want from her?

The counter lifting pulls my thoughts, and Rach, still dressed in her work clothes, meets me at the table. I just sit there for a moment, take in her beauty and her eyes grow big again.

"What? Do I have sauce on my face?"

"No, you just look beautiful."

She rolls her eyes at me. "Let's go."

I stand, capture her hand, and we step outside. This time we both do a quick check of the streets. Yeah, it must just be her paranoia rubbing off. "So about this job. You get harassed by assholes like those frat boys a lot?"

"Every night."

"I've been thinking. You've been doing such a good job around the house, and helping with Cassie, that I'd like to hire you." She gives me a strange look and I hurry on with, "I was going to hire someone. I just never found the time and I'm careful who I bring in to my house."

"I can understand that."

"I'll continue to look, but in the meantime, we'd love it if you stayed on."

She puckers her lips in thought. "How long are you thinking?"

I give a casual shrug. "Maybe until your finish classes in April. Then you'll have time to help me find a replacement, someone good enough."

She jerks her thumb over her shoulder as we walk. "I was planning to quit this job by then anyway."

"So that's a yes?"

"I..."

"The pay and hours will be better."

"No late-night shifts?"

"Your nights are yours to do with as you please."

She grins up at me. "That sounds...interesting."

"Oh they will be."

She hugs herself when the wind picks up and I throw my arm around her and drag her close. We hurry home, and she takes a quick shower and changes into her jeans and a sweater.

"Where are we going?" she asks.

"To Jericho's. Grab a bite and a drink, shoot some pool."

"Didn't you say that was on the wrong side of town?"

"You're with me, Rach. I told you, I'd never let anything happen to you."

I pull her close, and drops a soft kiss onto her mouth.

"Let's go."

I grab her coat, help her into it, and we head out into the night. She relaxes into the seat, and I smile. I like seeing her like this.

"It's nice to get out," she says on a soft sigh.

"Do you like to play pool?"

"I can't say as I ever played."

"What? Are you serious?" I ask.

"I guess my youth wasn't as misguided as yours."

I wink at her. "We'll have to see about fixing that."

A chuckle rumbles in her throat. "Great, first you're a distraction, now you're going to corrupt me."

"I believe I already have corrupted you," I say and slide a hand across the seat. I give her thigh a squeeze, and catch her mischievous look in the dashboard lights. What the hell is going on inside that brain of hers? I'm not sure, but when I get her home to my *empty* house, I plan to strip her bare and find out. I drive for another fifteen minutes, then pull into a dark parking lot.

"Stay put," I say, and climbs from the car. I catch her glancing into the dark night. Yeah, it's not the kind of neighborhood she usually hangs out in, but she has nothing to worry about when she's with me. I open her door, and hold my hand out to her. She takes it and smiles up at me.

"Wow, such a gentleman."

"I've been called a lot of things, babe, but that was never one of them."

She grins as I pull her close to protect her from the cold wind. I guide her to the doors, and music reaches our ears when I grab the brass handle and pull. The scent of beer, perfume and fried food falls over me, and beside me Rachel goes perfectly still for a second, her gaze cataloguing the room. I look at the room from her point of view, take in the big, tattooed guys hunkered over the pool table in the back. My gaze moves to a group of couples sharing a table and laughing over drinks. There are a few women hanging around, trying to get the attention of the guys playing pool. Behind the counter, I catch sight of Marissa, Jericho's wife. She meets my gaze and her smile widens.

I put my mouth close to Rachel's ear. "You okay?"

She nods to assure me, but I'm not so assured.

"Hey, if you don't want to stay."

"No, I do. I want to meet your friends, and play some pool."

"Get over here and give me a hug," Marissa says. I capture Rachel's hand to lead her across the scratched and pitted floor.

"Hey, Marissa. Good to see you." She leans over the counter to give me a big hug.

"Good to see you too." Her eyes narrow. "You look different, Jaxon."

I scrub my face. "Different good or different bad?"

"Definitely good." Marissa turns her eyes to Rachel. "Something tells me this sweet girl might be responsible for that."

She blushes a little at that, and she looks so goddam sweet, I can't help but wonder why we're at Jericho's instead of home between the sheets.

Why did you bring her here?

"I don't know about that?" Rachel says.

"Marissa, this is Rachel. She's my..."

Marissa has one curious eye on me, and the other on Rachel as she gives her a hug.

"I'm his next door neighbor," Rachel pipes in. "And I help out with Cassie."

"Cassie is such a doll, isn't she?" Marissa says

"She totally is. She's so funny, too. You should have heard her telling me about the way her dad ruins all her ponytails."

I stand back, dumbfounded at the fast bond between the two women. Then again, none of this should surprise me. Rachel is easy to like and Marissa loves everyone.

She didn't love Sarah.

"Get your fucking ass over here, so I can beat it."

Rachel turns at the sound of someone yelling to me from across the room. I laugh and rolls my eyes. "That's Sam. Don't mind him. He's still hurting from the time I handed him his ass on the end of a pool stick." I glance at Marissa, about to order some food and drinks, but she puts her hand up to stop me.

"A party platter, and two drinks coming up. A beer for you, Jaxon. What can I get for you, Rachel? How about a glass of white wine?"

"Actually, I think I'll have a beer, too."

"Now that's my kind of girl," Marissa says.

"Come and meet Sam," I say to her, and glance around looking for Jericho. "Hey Marissa, where's your husband?"

She gestures with her head to the back room. "Restocking. He'll be out in a second and I'm sure he'll be glad to see you both." She gives me a little eyebrow wave like she knows something I don't.

I lead Rachel across the room. "What's up, Sam?" I ask, and we lean in for a hug.

"Well, hey there," Sam says, and steps around me to see Rachel. "Are you lost?" I shake my head at his antics. He's a good guy, but a big fucking player.

He takes Rachel's hand in his, and she casts a hesitant glance my way. I recognize the look. It was the same one she gave me the day I helped her with her car. I smile at her to let her know Sam is one of the good guys, and she has nothing to fear from him. But as I watch her, my protective instincts kick in and once again, I fight the urge to hunt down the bastard that hurt her.

"I'm not lost? I'm here with—"

Sam jerks his thumb over his shoulder. "This guy?" He puts his hand over his heart, like he's wounded. "Tell me it isn't so. This guy is nothing but trouble."

"Maybe I like trouble," she says, relaxing into a playful conversation with my buddy.

"Oh, well then," he says, changing tactic, as he pours on the charm. "I'm way more trouble than he is."

She laughs. "I think you're way more everything than he is," she jabs back, not falling for his charm like nearly every other woman who's ever entered the place.

You tell him, Rach.

I smile at my girl, and her quick wit. She comes across as quiet and keeps her head down but she can be feisty when she wants to be—a girl who fights for what she believes in.

Does she believe in me? Would Cassie and I be enough to keep her around?

It's just an affair, dude?

The song playing in the background changes, and he take's Rachel's hand and spins her. "I'm a way better dancer, that's for sure."

Sam is kidding, I get that, but seeing his hands on Rachel sets me into motion. I remove Sam's hand from hers, and pull her close to me

"All right, that's enough. She came with me and she's leaving with me."

The door opens and in walks a couple of my old buddies, Jaret and Beck. They're razzing each other about something as they come my way, but their laughter fades when they see me standing beside Rachel, with possession written all over me, no doubt.

"Jaxon, what the fuck?" Jaret asks, as he fist pumps me.

"Hey Jaret," I say, then fist pump Beck, whose gaze keeps bobbing between Rachel and me. And why wouldn't he be looking at us like that? I've not been with anyone since Sarah. Not anyone I was serious about, anyway.

Oh, fuck me.

"You want to put your eyes back in your head or would you prefer me to do it for you," I say to Beck, and give him a playful punch to the shoulder. Beck shakes his head at me, and I continue with, "Now say hello to Rachel, so we can get to the game of pool I promised her."

Rachel stares at my friends like she doesn't know what to make of them. They all exchange pleasantries, and Marissa comes by with our food and drinks. She sets them on the table, and then whacks Sam's hand when he reaches for a mozzarella stick.

"Hey," she says. "Keep your hands to yourself, these are for my new friend." She smiles at Rachel and saunters away.

Rachel laughs when Sam gives her a wounded look. "You can have my mozzarella stick," she says, plucking one from the tray and handing it over.

"I like her, Jaxon," Sam says as he bites into the snack.

Me, too.

"Even if she does have bad taste in guys."

I laugh.

"You like any girl who gives you food." I nudge Rachel. "Come on, let's play."

She takes a sip of her beer, and grabs an onion ring as I rack the balls. Beside us, Sam and Beck start a game as Jaret goes and gets the drinks.

"I like your friends," she says to me.

"Yeah?" I was hoping she would. "They like you too." I was hoping for that too.

"Do you all go way back?"

"As far as I can remember."

A melancholy look crosses her face. "That's so nice."

I grab two pool cues and hand one to her. "Do you still have childhood friends?"

Her expression changes, becomes almost stricken. "No, I didn't really..." she glances at the pool table, like she's looking for a distraction, and I take that opportunity to change the subject.

"Okay, this is how we put the chalk on the cue." I do mine then hand it to her. My gaze rakes over her face, and I fucking hate that she has so many demons. I know it's not my business, but goddammit, I want her to talk to me.

"I'll break," I say. I position the white cue ball, and crack the balls. I sink two low, and explain the rules to her as I move around the table, sinking a few more.

"Hey, you're pretty good at this."

"Not as good as me," Sam says and Rachel laughs as she offers him up another mozzarella stick. We both take a sip of beer, and I teach her how to hold the stick for her shot. She bends over the table, and a groan I have no control over crawls out of my throat.

"You okay over there, buddy?" Jaret asks.

"Fine."

"Sounds like you're having a *hard* time," Sam pipes in accentuating the word hard, and the guys all start laughing.

Clowns, every one of them.

Why again did I bring Rachel here?

"Hey, Marissa said you were out here," Jericho says, coming up to give me a hug as Rachel takes her shot. My friend has that same look in his eyes from the day he stopped at my place. I never did get to ask him what was going on.

She makes her shot and beams at me. "Must be beginner's luck."

"Maybe I'm a good teacher."

"I'm a better teacher," Sam pipes in.

"So this must be the neighbor you told me about," Jericho says, and smiles at Rachel.

Rachel looks a bit alarmed. "You...told your friend about me?"

Instead of answering, I say, "Rachel, this is Jericho." I pat my buddy on the shoulder. "I probably wouldn't be where I am today if it wasn't for him."

"Nah, you'd have been just fine," Jericho says, but we both know that's not true. "He's like a cat. He always lands on his feet." I stare at my buddy. Is he talking about Sarah leaving me? Fuck, I never thought I'd get over that, that my world would have righted itself again.

Sam takes a shot and grunts. "Jaxon won't let his new girl-friend play with us."

"I don't blame him," Jericho say.

"She's only with him because he saw her first."

"Sam, shut the hell up," Jericho says and shakes his head.

"Even if she wasn't with him, something tells me she's too smart for your bullshit."

Sam pouts and grins at Rachel as he points to an onion ring. She nods and he scoops it up and tosses it into his mouth.

"It's nice to meet you, Rachel." He takes her hand in his. "Jaxon was very lucky he met you first." He turns to me and winks, and it's ridiculous how happy I am that she fits in here with the guys I think of as family. "You're lucky I didn't find her first."

From the corner of my eye, I catch the alarm on Rachel's face. Jericho is still looking at me when he lowers his voice and says, "Can I speak to you in private for a moment."

RACHEL

Rachel

It's late by the time we finally make it home. I stifle a yawn as I exit the car, and glance at my house. At least tonight's party hasn't spilled out onto the lawn. The cold weather must be keeping them all inside. I glance up to my bedroom, and it's pitch dark. A smile touches my mouth. It was so thoughtful of Jaxon to put a lock on my door. Not that I've been spending a heck of a lot of time in there.

As I meet Jaxon at the front of the car, I give more thought to his offer. While I'd like to quite Pizza Villa, is spending more time with him smart? I always prided myself on my intellect, but the things I've been doing lately...well, not conducive to keeping a low profile and my brain focused only on school.

"Tired?" Jaxon asks.

"It's been a long day."

"Let's get you inside and into bed. You could use a good night's sleep."

It was true. I did need sleep, but I have no idea how much time I'll have left with this man and I want to make the most of it. After Mom died and I was left with my father, I didn't have the luxury of feeling safe, or just letting go. Then my ex came along, and I found myself in another bad situation. But with Jaxon, he's big and strong—much like the abusive guys in my life—but he's caring and protective, and doesn't frighten me at all. In fact, everything about him warms and comforts me, which has my thoughts racing to the bag I packed earlier.

We step inside the house and the noise next door dulls as we shut the world out. "How about a drink before bed," I say as we walk shed our coats.

"Sure. Beer or wine?"

"I think I'll have a glass of wine." I go up on my toes and kiss him.

As his mood changes, his eyes dim with desire. "What was that for?"

"I had fun tonight, even though your friend Sam is a little crazy."

He laughs. "That's one word for it."

"I'll be right back."

Cupboards open and close, followed by the fridge as I hurry down the hallway. I grab my bag and slip into Jaxon's bedroom. I draw his curtains, then hurry into the cute outfit I borrowed from my roommate. I examine myself in the mirror. Sylvie should be happy to know her costume was definitely going to get some action.

I crack the door and pad quietly down the hall, I peek into the kitchen but Jaxon isn't there. With one hand behind my back, I take a few more steps and find him sitting on the sofa, a remote in one hand as he flicks through the stations, a beer in the other.

Without looking up he says, "Anything you want to watch?"

"Not really. Anything you'd like to watch?"

His head lifts, and the remote in his hands falls with a clatter to the floor. "Jesus Christ." I grin at the heat in his eyes, the way his hand is shaking a bit as he sets his beer down. "There is definitely something I want to watch," he says, his voice deeper as he crooks his finger to gesture me over.

"What's that?"

"I want to watch my cock sliding in and out of you."

A burst of heat zings through me, and I hurry to him. He spreads his legs, and I stand between them. "I told you not to wear this." His hunger vibrates through me.

"But I thought you'd like it," I tease.

"Oh, I like it. I like it so goddamn much I'm not going to be able to control myself, Rach. I'm going to fucking ruin you." He pushes his finger into my mouth. "It makes me want to tie you to the bed and destroy this pretty mouth."

"Maybe that's exactly why I wore it."

He goes perfectly still. "Rach?"

I pull my hand out from behind my back, and produce two long pieces of ribbon. Jaxon's breathing changes, becomes hard. "Tie me to your bed, Jaxon. Destroy my mouth."

Without so much as a word he stands, and lifts me onto his hips. I wrap my legs and arms around him as he carries me down the hall, kicking his bedroom door shut with his foot. He settles me on the bed, and stands back, his hot gaze perusing my sexy outfit. I inch my legs open, just to tease him a bit more and a deep rumble reverberates through the room.

He tears his shirt off and makes quick work of his pants. As he stands before me completely naked, I can't help but think I won the man lottery. He's beautiful. Big. Strong. A tough body inked with art, but he'd never do anything to hurt me.

You are not walking away from this unscathed, Rachel.

I settle on the bed, and spread my arms. His brow furrows for a second. I study him, take in his posture, the narrowing of his eyes. He thinks this is hard for me, that I'm only doing this for him. I appreciate his concern. But this isn't just for him. It's for me too.

"I trust you," I say, and his entire body softens. Well, not his entire body. There is still one part of him that's rock hard.

"Rach," he whispers, and steps up to me. He slides one hand down my side, brushing my outer breast. Deft fingers tug at the band on my garter, and when he sees I'm wearing stockings, sans panties, his gaze shoots to mine.

"You are so beautiful." He runs his hands along my garter until he reaches my lace stockings. "These stay on." His hand slides back up to the lace holding the bosom of the short dress together. "So does this." He unties the lace until my breasts are exposed, then lays over me.

His mouth settles over mine, and I widen my legs as he reaches for my hands and puts them over my head. "All mine," he whispers as he buries his face in my neck. "All night. Everything and anything I want."

I'm not sure if he's asking permission or not, so I answer with, "Yesss, please." The eagerness in my voice does something to him. He presses fast, open mouth kisses to my throat, my chin, my lip, then widens his legs around my body. He sits up, and shifts until his cock is inches from my mouth.

I moan, eager to take him, but he has other idea in mind. He takes my arms and spread them, then with slow easy movements—likes he's giving me time to change my mind—he ties me to the bedpost.

"Yes," I whisper again, just to let him know how sure I am about this—about him.

He settles himself between my spread legs and goes back on his knees. He takes a long time to examine his handiwork. His eyes are full of adoration and worship when they finally meet mine, and my heart misses a beat.

"Jaxon," I finally manage to say after he swallows hard.

"Yeah, baby?" he asks slowly, quietly, like he's gone to a different place in his head.

"I want you."

"I want you, too," he says, and leans forward to cover my sex with is mouth.

"Oh, Jaxon," I cry out as he devours me like a man starved for so much more than just sex. I move my hips and he slides one hand under my ass to lift it. With my body better positioned for what he's doing to me, he slides his tongue over me, inside me, and I'm already soaring, ready and willing to go anywhere this man wants to take me.

He inserts a finger and I'm done for. "That is so good," I say, and clench around him. Each sweet pulse of pleasure takes me higher, until I'm freefalling without a net, but Jaxon is there to catch me, of that I'm sure.

He laps at me, drinks my every drop like a man dying of thirst. I move against his mouth, wet his entire face with my liquid heat. When I stop spasming, he slides up my body and I taste myself on his tongue when his lips crash over mine. He kisses me hard, deep, then spreads his legs and goes up on his knees.

"Open that pretty mouth of yours," he commands.

I do as he says and he feeds me his cock. It hits the back of my throat and I choke a little, but I continue to take him deeper. I never loved a man's cock in my mouth until Jaxon. Now I can't get enough of it.

"I love watching you take me like this," he growls, and his cock thickens impossibly more in my mouth. I wiggle my tied hands, wanting to touch him all over, but they're restrained. A strange thrill goes through me. My God, I've come so far so fast under this man's care. "That's it, take me deep. Show me how much you love my cock."

His dirty words turn me on even more and I writhe beneath him, wanting him inside my body again. He must sense it, because he pulls out, slides over me and in one quick thrust drives his cock into me, seating himself high.

"This where you want my cock?" he asks.

"Yeah," I say, and move my hips. He pumps into me. "I want your cock in me, everywhere."

He stills for a brief second, then picks up the pace again. "Everywhere?"

"Yes."

"You ready for that?" he asks quietly.

"I'm ready for everything with you, Jaxon."

With that he pulls out of my sex and reaches up to untie my hands. I catch the intensity in his eyes and nearly forget how to breathe.

"In my bag," I say. "I brought lubricant."

His eye latch onto mine. "You planned this?"

"Yes."

"You're full of surprises, babe," he says softly. He reaches into my bag and produces the lubricant. He places it on the nightstand, grips my hips and flips me over. Warm fingers trail down my spine, and I quiver.

"Take me, Jaxon."

"Oh, I plan to," he groans, and slides a pillow under my hips to lift my ass to him. I should feel vulnerable and exposed, but I don't. He kneads my ass for a few moments, as he presses hungry kisses to my back.

My body goes cold when he shifts, moving off me to grab the lubricant. The top flips open and he peels the foil off.

"This might be a bit cold," he murmurs as he presses a finger into me.

"Ohmigod," I murmur against the coldness and the pressure.

He stops moving. "You okay, babe?"

"Yes, more." I wiggle to encourage him and his agonized groan makes me smile. I like being here with Jaxon like this. I like what we're doing, and the way he makes me feel as I give myself to him in a way I've never given myself to anyone.

You weren't supposed to give him your heart, Rach.

But that thought is for another time. Right now, I need to concentrate on the way he's taking his time with me, preparing, widening, stretching me for his girth. He plays with me for a long time, but I'm ready for him. I just know my body will adjust to his. We're such a good fit together.

"Please," I whisper.

He lifts my hips a bit more and positions himself. I suck in a sharp breath as he presses his crown into me. I tighten, and he stops.

"Am I hurting you?"

I try to relax, and when I do, the pain subsides a little. "No," I say. "I want to feel you inside me."

He goes slow, inching in and then giving me time to catch up. We continue this for a long time, and when he's finally all the way inside me, he lets loose a groan unlike anything I've ever heard before.

"Now I've been everywhere inside you," he says, so much pleasure in his voice my heart squeezes.

He moves his hips slowly, and I get used to the pressure. His chest presses against my back as he lays over me and kisses my neck. As he applies weight, my hard nipples press against the sheets, and the stimulation races to the needy spot between my legs. Jackson moves, a little more urgency with each thrust now and I love the hot little grunting sounds he's making in my ear.

He shoves a hand between my body and the pillow, and presses his finger to my clit. I exhale hard as pleasure centers on my sex. My body rocks as he thrusts, and my clit grinds harder against his finger.

"I'm..." My words fall off as a mind-exploding orgasm rockets me into space. I close my eyes against the flood of heat, and pant, desperate to catch my breath. Jaxon grunts again, and my entire body burns as he fills me with his hot cum.

He collapses, and presses all his weight on top of me. I can't breathe, but I don't care. I've never felt closer to anyone in my entire life. Jaxon shifts slightly and pulls out of me, and I instantly miss him inside my body.

"Are you okay?" he whispers into my ear as he gently brushes my damp hair from my face.

"Define okay?" I ask and he laughs.

"I'll get us water. Don't move."

I stretch out on the bed, and remove the pillow from beneath me. His bare feet slap the floor as he rushes down the hall. I rake my nails though the sheets, a content cat stretching. I think I might even be purring, too. That makes me chuckle.

"Something funny?" he asks and when I roll over, catch sight of his cute dimple, my damn heart can barely take it.

"Not really. Just thinking about how good I feel."

He hands me a glass of water, and touches my face. "Yeah, you do feel good."

I take a big drink and wet my parched throat, and he takes the glass from me and finishes it.

"More?" he asked.

"I'm good."

"Shower?"

"That would be perfect, but my legs aren't moving."

"I got you," he says and scoops me up. He carries me to the shower, adjusts the temperature and climbs in with me. I'm so lethargic, I'm sure I'm going to fall asleep in his arms. Once we're clean, he turns the water off, and covers me in a big fluffy towel. I catch my second breath as we exit the bathroom.

"Want to finish your wine, or straight to bed?" he asks.

"Let's sit in the living room for a bit. See what's on TV."

He ties his towel at his waist and we stay close as we move down the hall. I examine his living room before I sit, and smile when I see a few of Cassie's toys laying around. Jaxon flicks the TV on, and I snuggle in next to him. He flicks through the channels, but when I look up at him, I find him looking back.

"Rach?" he begins.

"Yeah?"

"Tonight at the bar, when Jericho said I was lucky he didn't find you first. You seemed really put off by that."

I sit up, cross my legs and face him. "He's a married man."

Jaxon touches my face, and I lean into his warm palm. It's rough from years of manual labor yet warm and gentle against my skin. "He's was only kidding, babe. He and Marissa are totally in love." I look down at my lap as painful memories bubble to the surface. "What is it?" he asks so quietly, so damn affectionately, that for the first time I feel that maybe here, with him to anchor me, I can talk about the past. I close my eyes and take a breath. It wasn't as steady as I'd have liked, but when I blow it out and open my eyes again, Jaxon is there, patient and calm. I draw from that and begin.

"My father..." I pause for one second, then go on. "He was an alcoholic. A mean one at times."

He shifts closer, and lets his hands drop to the towel covering my legs. His thumb moves gently over the terry cloth. Soothing. "I'm sorry."

I nod, and swallow hard. Tears burn my eyes. Here I thought I'd never cry over my father again. "Mom tried to protect me from the things he used to do, but she couldn't."

"Can you tell me what he did?" Jaxon asks softly. His hand moves up and closes over mind. A simple touch, yet the strength that flows into me from that gentle caress fills me with the courage to go on.

"So many weekends he'd disappear. Mom would keep me busy to keep my mind off it, but I always felt the tension she tried to hide from me. I'd see her smile falter when she thought I wasn't looking." I pause as a tightness grips my stomach, and my throat fills with acid. "He'd stumble home on Sunday, the same clothes he left in and smelling like cheap perfume." I pull my gaze from his and look over his shoulder as the past rises up and engulfs me. "I hated those women, Jaxon, almost as much as I hated my father. I didn't know who they were, had never laid eyes on them, but I *hated* them." My other hand lifts, palm up. Empty. I look back at him. "How could he leave his family and sleep with other women? How could they sleep with a man who was married?" A sob catches in my throat and spills from my lips. Jaxon's hand on my leg tightens. "I hated how much that hurt Mom, you know." I look away again and dab at my eyes, and fighting back the tears.

"It's okay to cry for your mother, Rach." A long pause and then, "It's okay to cry for you, too. What your father did was pretty shitty. A girl needs her Dad." I glance at him and it dawns on me that he's talking from experience. "He's her first true love, and it's up to him to set a good example and show her how she's supposed to be treated by guys."

A noise crawls out of my throat, a half laugh, half cry. "I guess that's why I ended up in a relationship with Dylan."

"Dylan?" he asks, and brushes my tear away with his thumb.

"My ex. He was...so much like my father."

"He hurt you?"

There is real pain in Jaxon's eyes as his gaze searches my face. Behind that pain is also anger. My body quivers, almost violently. "Yes, he hurt me," I whisper. "He was violent, and he threatened to kill me if I left him, or went to the cops. I was terrified."

His teeth clench and the sound reverberates through me. "Where is he?"

I shake my head. I'm not going to let Jaxon put himself, or his daughter in harm's way for me. Nothing good could come from it, of that I'm sure. "Not around here."

Jaxon's eyes narrow, turning the strangest shade of blue, as his eyes narrow. "Does he know where you are?"

"No."

He relaxes a bit, and so do I. "He was so nice at first, and I was a little flattered that he liked me. I usually have my head down and fly under the radar, you know?"

"I know you keep your head down, Rach, but you hardly fly under the radar. You were on mine the second you moved in next door."

"Oh," I say, totally surprised by that.

"So you never liked to be noticed, even before Dylan."

I shake my head and Jaxon peels a wet strand of hair from my forehead when it sticks. "I wanted to make something of myself, be independent. I never wanted to find myself in a position like my Mom, stuck in an abusive relationship, with no way out. And I want to protect all the children."

"You are an amazing woman."

The corner of my mouth turns up. "Thank you."

"You showed up here in the middle of the night. No family, barely any luggage, always looking over your shoulder. I pretty much figured out you were on the run."

"His threats were getting more violent, so I summoned all my courage and went to the police. Turns out there were some outstanding charges against him in other states. They were going to arrest him, and I knew he'd come after me for that. I had no choice but to leave."

"You did good, Rachel."

I slide my fingers through his. "I'm still scared."

He shifts closer and turns me, until my head is rests on his shoulders. "I won't let anything happen to you."

"He's dangerous, Jaxon."

"So am I." He absently runs his fingers up and down my arm. His touch is like a healing balm and a sense of security that I haven't felt in...ever, falls over me. "Tell me about your mom."

"She died of cancer. She swallowed down my father's betrayal and I think it killed her from the inside out."

"What else did you two do, besides knit together?"

I sit up again, and meet his eyes. I miss my mother more than words can say, but as I conjure up the happy times we had, warmth soothes my soul. "You would have loved her."

"If she was anything like the amazing daughter she raised, then yeah, I would."

"She tried to make my childhood as normal as possible. Every Sunday we'd bake these cookies. Ohmigod, Jackson they were so good. Just a simple sugar cookie, but I can almost taste them now." He smiles at that.

"That's a great memory, Rach."

"After baking, we'd go to the park, have a picnic, fly a kite. We didn't have a lot but she'd always have those little gummy green leaf mints for me as a treat."

He groans. "I haven't had one of those in years."

I lean against him again and let the happier memories push out the demons. My eyes slide shut, exhaustion from a long day and even longer night pulling me under.

"Rach?"

"Yeah."

"You never did tell me what you wanted for your birthday."

"One more day with my mom," I whisper.

A lifetime with you.

14

JAXON

Jaxon

Jaxon

It's Sunday afternoon and upstairs, the sound of Cassie's feet running down the hall, followed by Rachel's, put a big smile on my face. I put my wrench away and glance at the calendar hanging over my workbench. We're halfway through November which means it's been two weeks since we were at Jericho's pub, two weeks since he warned me that Sarah was finally clean, and coming home. Apparently, as Jericho explained, Jessica had stopped into the bar and he overheard her telling a friend that she'd texted Sarah about my new *freshman*—Jessica's words, not Jericho's.

But I'll believe it when I see it and while I've always wanted Sarah in Cassie's life, Rachel, Cassie and I have fallen into an easy routine. Rachel left her job and has been helping me out around here. We fall in bed together every night, and every morning we get up well before Cassie and carry on as if there is nothing going on between us—that what we have is a business arrangement only—with a few added perks, of course. Only problem is, I want more going on between us, which has my thoughts drifting back to the night she opened up to me. She's still afraid of her ex, which means she could so easily run again. But no way is he going to find her here, right? And if he does, he'll have me to deal with.

Then again, are we even enough for her to stick around?

The door to my shop opens and in walks my in-laws. My head rears back in surprise. There are no plans for them to take Cassie today, but they've been known to stop by unexpectedly from time to time. Likely to try and catch me off guard so they can find some reason to take Cassie away from me.

"Judy, Karl," I begin. "What a pleasant surprise. Cassie is upstairs if you're looking for her."

"Actually, we're here to talk to you," Karl says as he slowly approaches.

I grab a rag, wipe the grease from my hand, and ignore the knot tightening in my stomach. Something is very wrong here, but I keep a poker face and gesture to the two clean chairs.

"Have a seat, or would you rather go upstairs?" I ask, and point to the ceiling.

"Here is fine," Judy says and brushes the chair to check the cleanliness of it before she sits.

"Have you heard from Sarah?" Karl asks, getting right to the point.

"Not since that text over three weeks ago."

He eyes me carefully, waiting for a reaction when he says, "She's coming back."

Giving no indication on whether I think that is a good thing, or a bad thing, I lean against the counter and my mind races. Why now after all this time? Was it really because I was with another woman? Why would she even care? She was the one who chose to leave us. It wasn't the other way around.

"When?" I ask.

Karl hesitates and I resist the urge to scoff, because yeah, his pause tells me he's as skeptical as I am. "She said soon."

Like I said, I'll believe it when I see it.

"Jaxon, I was just wondering if you wanted..." Halfway down the stairs, Rachel stops speaking and blinks. "Oh, sorry, I didn't realize you had company."

"Rachel," Judy says tightly, like the name has left a bad taste in her mouth. Rachel freezes, and anger shoots through me. They can treat me however the hell they want but they're not going to be mean to Rachel.

"Is there a problem, Judy?" I ask between clenched teeth.

She touches her beads. "No, it's just." She turns her attention from me to Rachel. "Cassie's mother is coming home, and well..."

"Well, what?" I ask, bringing her eyes back to me.

"I...should go. Cassie wants her hair braided."

"What did you want to ask me, Rachel?"

She hesitates for a second then says, "I'm making lunch and was wondering if you wanted a ham or chicken sandwich."

"Whatever you make is fine with me."

Rachel turns to go, and I focus back in on Judy.

"I don't like that girl trying to be Cassie's mother," Judy says quickly, her lips pinched so tight they accentuate the lines on her lips, a gentle reminder that this has all been hard on her too. "Not when she has her own."

"Cassie's never had a mother, Judy. Not since the day she was born," I say flatly, honestly, wanting to get the point across, without gutting her. The truth is Judy is angry, angry that Rachel is here and her daughter isn't, but no way am I going to let her direct her feelings at the wrong woman. Rachel has been nothing but good to us.

"She's all Cassie talks about, Jaxon," Judy shoots back. "It's not healthy. That child needs stability. Not some barely legal girl who's going to breeze out of your life as easily as she breezed into it. What do you really know about her, anyway?"

It takes everything in my not to hit something. "Like you, I wish Sarah was in our lives, but she's not and we're doing the best to make a go at it," I say, refusing to discuss Rachel with her. Rachel deserves better than that from me.

The stairs creak, a splitting little sound that races down my spine. I jerk my head around and catch sight of Rachel's ankles before she closes the upstairs door.

"Jaxon," Karl begins.

"If you want to see Cassie, take her out for a few hours, I'm sure she'd love that."

Two sets of eyes stare at me in shock. I rarely push back, after all, they lost a daughter in all this, but I've just about had enough of their bullshit.

"We'd love to spend the day with her," Karl says, then lowers his voice and adds, "Thank you."

"You're welcome," I say. Clearly, on some level, they understand I could keep Cassie from them if I wanted. But I'd only be hurting my child, and I'd never in a million years want to do that to her.

I hurry up the stairs, and go down the hall in search of Cassie. She'll be happy to know her grandparents are here. My steps slow when I hear voices coming from her room.

"Rachel," Cassie begins quietly, in that mature voice reserved for when she has something important to say. I want her to remain an innocent child for as long as possible, but there are times I realize she's more grown up than I'd like.

"Yeah, kiddo," Rachel says using my nickname for my daughter. It brings a smile to my face.

"Grandma and Grandpa told me my mommy is going to come home."

Rage goes through me. Fuck, man, they had no right to

say that to her, or get her hopes up in any way. I make a mental note to have a little talk to them when I go back downstairs. I'm about to enter the room, but stop when Rachel stills, and I get the sense she stopped breathing.

"I...heard. That's great news, Cassie." I catch sight of my two girls sitting on the bed, Rachel combing out her hair.

Cassie scrunches her face up the way she always does when she's deep in thought. "But I want you to be my mommy, Rachel."

15
RACHEL

As November bleeds into December, there has been no sign of Sarah and I'm not sure how I feel about that. Cassie said she wanted me to be her mother, but Jaxon flat out said to his in-laws that he wishes Sarah was back in their lives. My mind races back to that day on Cassie's bed, when she made that statement. I was shocked by her words, maybe even more shocked to glance up and see Jaxon in the doorway. He had a strange look on his face, one I'd never seen before. I must have had that same look on my face, because the one thing we didn't want happening was, well...happening. Cassie was growing close to me, looking at me as a mother figure, and that was something we'd been trying to avoid.

But I want that.

Jaxon still loves his ex.

My stomach cramps at that. I am so freaking stupid. This was just supposed to be an affair. I wasn't supposed to fall for this man or his daughter.

I flip the page on my textbook, and try to concentrate, but the house is quiet, too quiet. A loud bang sounds outside

—something like a trash can tipping over—and I glance up from Jaxon's kitchen table. It's mid-week, and there are no parties going on at my place. I laugh at that. *My place.* I'm paying rent for a room I barely use. I walk quietly across the floor and glance out into the darkness. My heart jumps into my throat when I see movement near the bushes. I leap back, and take a few deep breaths. When will I ever stop worrying that my ex has found me?

Probably never.

I take a few quick breaths to calm myself and check the clock. It's nearing seven, but with the days growing shorter, the nights are that much longer—and darker. It's a school night, which means Jaxon and Cassie should be back soon. They've been disappearing a couple times a week. Daddy/daughter things, Jaxon explained, without telling where they've been and really, is it any of my business?

Heck, maybe Sarah is back and they are sneaking out to see her. As old insecurities and fears creep their way back in, I push them down. Jaxon is a good man. He'd never do something so devious. Right? Besides, Cassie would come straight out and tell me that she's been seeing her mom. That little girl doesn't have a dishonest bone in her body. But then again, she's been acting a bit strange and secretive too.

A lump forms in my throat, and warning bells urge me to end this now. To stop playing house with Jaxon and his daughter. Yeah, I should close my books, pack up my clothes and head next door. Once there, I should give my room to one of the other girls to avoid seeing him moving around in his room shirtless.

So why aren't I doing any of that?

God, I am so pathetic.

I should leave. I should leave right now.

A car door slams followed by Cassie's voice. "Daddy, that was fun."

"It's our secret, remember?"

My heart falls into my stomach. Why do they have a secret? What is it that they don't want me to know? I'm not sure, but as a chill goes through me, I fold my arms across myself and hug.

They entered through the front door, and the second Jaxon sees me, he goes into warrior mode. "Rachel, what is it?"

God, what do I tell him? That I've fallen for him and his daughter. That I'd like to make what we're doing here permanent. I can't say those things. Jaxon asked me to stay on as the nanny and never spoken long term. How could he when his ex could walk through the door any day and ask for her family back?

I open my mouth, but when I hesitate, he comes toward me and puts both hands on my arms. I absorb his warmth, revel in it.

"I heard a noise outside earlier. It spooked me."

His brow furrows. "Yeah?"

"Yeah, there are no parties at my place, so it just freaked me out a bit."

"Okay, why don't you get Cassie in the bath, and I'll do a perimeter check. It was probably just a raccoon or something."

"Okay," I say, hating myself for feeling all emotional. He disappears outside, locking up behind him, and I take a look at Cassie. "Bath time."

She takes my hands and my heart wobbles as she skips down the hall. How could any mother leave a child like her? I pour the bath and help Cassie in.

Without wanting to pry too much, I ask. "So you had a fun with your daddy tonight?"

She smiles. "I had a lot of fun."

"I'm so glad." I want to ask here where she went and what

she did, but I don't want to betray Jaxon's trust. I help her bath, wash her hair, and by the time we're finished, Jaxon's footsteps coming down the all reach my ears.

"Hey," he says. "Let's get you into your pajamas." I hand over a clean Cassie to him and make my way back to my books. I flip the pages, so lost in thought I hadn't heard Jaxon's approach.

He touches my hair, and I nearly jump ten feet in the air.

"Whoa. You okay?" he asks.

"I didn't hear you."

He narrows his eyes. "What's bothering you?"

I make light of it, but I fear he can see right through me. "That noise spooked me," I say, not a lie, and gesture with a nod toward the window.

"It was nothing." He scrubs his chin, and averts my eyes. The hairs on my neck tingle. What is he not telling me. "Just a kicked over trash can. Raccoon likely." I'm about to question him on that, when he says. "Want to watch a movie?"

"I can't. Exams, and I'm having a hard time concentrating."

His grin turns mischievous. "You know I can help you with that."

I laugh, a little of the tension leaving with it. "I know, but my exam is tomorrow."

"When is your last exam?"

"December 9th."

"Ah, the day before your birthday."

"You remembered my birthday?"

He gives me a look like I'm dense. "Yeah. So about me helping you concentrate," he says, bringing the conversation back to sex.

Or is this about sex?

Maybe he really is interested in my school, and grades. He knows they are important to me, and he's been so supportive, driving me back and forth—even though my own car is working now—and making my lunches to ensure I'm fueling the brain. His words, not mine.

"I can't be up all night making love to you."

Making love.

Oh, God Rachel get it together.

A softness comes over him, and he says, "How about just half the night." He bends forward, presses his lips to mine. His kiss, so achingly tender and profound it takes me by surprise and has me wondering if he really is still in love with this ex. No man can kiss like that without feeling something more, right?

Do I dare hope?

"Okay, half the night," I agree.

16

JAXON

"Daddy, where is she?" Cassie asks impatiently from the back seat.

"She'll be here any second," I say, and scan the big steps leading to her lecture hall. I glance at the dashboard clock. Rachel's last exam before the Christmas break ended at five and it's ten minutes past. I tap my leg restlessly. I hope everything went all right for her. I've been helping her stay focused, but I hope I wasn't taking up too much of her time, or making her too tired when we fell into bed and made love every night.

"There she is, Daddy. There she is," Cassie yells, and I can't help but chuckle. When this affair started, it was with the intention of a sex-only relationship for me, and Cassie was never supposed to fall for the girl next door. Well, so much for best laid plans, because both of us are crazy about her, and tonight after I get Cassie tucked into bed, I'm going to tell her that.

A smile splits Rachel's face as she tugs on her dollar store mitts and hurries toward us. My heart beats a little fast when her gaze meets mine, and since she's smiling I can only hope her exams went well.

"Hey, you two," she says as she jumps into the passenger seat. "It's cold out there."

No matter how much I want to kiss her, I can't. Not before I talk to her tonight, and then to Cassie. My daughter is smart, and probably guesses how we feel about each other, but I want to have a conversation with her before we publicly display our affection. So instead of kissing her shivering mouth, I slide a hand across the seat and place it on her leg.

"How did it go?"

"Not too bad."

"Yeah."

"Pretty good, actually."

"That's my girl," I say, and give her leg a squeeze.

Cassie starts to kick my seat. "Let's go, Daddy." I laugh. She's so excited to finally show Rachel what we've secretly been doing the last week.

"What are you so excited about, Cassie?" Rachel asks.

I glance at my daughter in the rearview mirror and she take a deep breath and puffs her cheeks out, like she's been doing for the last few weeks when it took everything in her to keep our surprise from Rachel.

"I'm hungry," she finally blurts out.

"Oh, well as soon as we get home, I'll make us something to eat," Rachel says. I smile at that, the world as I know it right for the first time in a long time. She gives me a strange look. "What?" she asks me like I just grew a second head.

Instead of answering, I ease into traffic, and Cassie and Rachel chat. "What do you feel like having for dinner tonight, kiddo?"

"I...um..."

I catch Cassie's eyes in the mirror again. "Let's wait and see what's in the fridge when we get home."

"Why are you two acting so weird?" Rachel asks curiously, cautiously.

"We're not."

For a brief second she looks away, but not before I catch the concern on her face. Wanting to lighten her mood, I redirect the conversation. "So you must feel relieved now that Christmas break is here."

"We're getting our tree tomorrow," Cassie yells out from the back seat. "We're cutting it down ourselves."

"That's nice."

"We had to wait a long time this year," Cassie announces.

"Oh, why is that?" Rachel asks.

"Cassie," I say, a little warning in my voice. I don't want her to spill the reason we've been waiting. She puffs her cheeks out again and I glance at Rachel, catch that worried look again.

"It was a timing thing," I explain.

"Oh, I see." She folds her hand on her lap and stares straight ahead.

"Daddy, it's snowing," Cassie says, and I smile as I flick on the wipers to wash away the few flakes. This night couldn't be any more perfect.

Rachel is acting a little strange when we reach home. She climbs from the car and looks from my front door to hers, like she's debating on which direction to go. I give her a little nudge. She's been with us for over a month now. I have no idea why she would ever want to step back into her party house, and I'll ask her what's going on later when I sit her down for a talk, but for now, Cassie is going to burst from her secrets if we don't get inside.

I scoop Cassie up, grab Rachel's hand and hurry up the front steps. I unlock the door, and the second we step inside, Cassie yells, "Surprise."

I laugh at that. The poor kid has been doing so good, I

can't blame her for not being able to hold it for another second.

"What's going on?" Rachel asks as I flick the lights on. The scent of sugar cookies reaches our nostrils and Rachel breathes in deep. "You baked?"

"We baked," Cassie says, and I set her down. She grabs Rachel's hand. "Come on."

I follow behind as Cassie ushers Rachel down the hall and into the kitchen. When Rachel enters, she goes perfectly still. I step up behind her, put my mouth to her ear.

"Happy birthday, Rach."

She takes in the table set for three. Yeah, I had to read up on how to properly set a table, but Rachel is so worth the effort, but it will never make up for the things my daughter is learning from her.

She spins to face me, and blinks rapidly, but I see the water in her eyes. "This is for me?"

"For your birthday."

"It's not until tomorrow."

"But we wanted to celebrate early."

"Why?"

Because I couldn't wait one more minute to tell her how I feel and ask her to stay here with us both permanently.

"It's a timing thing," I say without any further explanation.

She pinches her lips tight and turns from us. "You made my favorite sugar cookies."

"Not sure if they're the same recipe as your mom's, but we tried. And there is cake in the fridge in case we messed up."

Cassie giggles at that. "We made lasagna, too."

"My favorite," she says quietly.

"I know," I murmur from behind.

"How did you know?"

"There is a lot I know, Rachel, and we need to talk after, okay?"

Before she can respond, Cassie grabs a chair and pulls it out. "Sit, Rachel."

I walk around Rachel and wave my hand. "For the lady," I say and she grins as she lowers herself. "Cassie and I will be serving you tonight."

Cassie grabs the bowl with the rolls and places them on the table, and I fill three wine glasses. Two with white wine, and one with apple juice. Rachel is quiet as I fill our plates with food, and set them down.

"You okay?" I ask.

"I can't believe you two sneaks did this." Cassie laughs. "Is this why you've been going out twice a week?"

"Nope," Cassie says. "Daddy, can we? Can we?" she says, her voice getting higher and higher.

"Yeah, sure, Cassie. You've waited long enough."

Cassie squeals, darts into the other room and comes back with a poorly wrapped present for Rachel.

"Cassie, this is amazing. Did you wrap this?" she asks.

"Ah, no I did," I say and Rachel laughs.

"Good job, Jaxon," she teases, her voice light and playful like she's talking to a puppy who'd just been house-broken.

"Open it!" Cassie squeals.

"Okay, okay." She tears into the package, and my heart lodges in my throat when I see the wide-eyed, glassy way Rachel is staring at the gift.

"We made them," Cassie says, but I'm guessing she doesn't need to tell Rachel that, judging by the mismatched badly knitted pair of mittens in her hands.

"Ohmigod," she says on a sob. "I...I..." she begins and swallows like she can't get the words out. "This is what you guys have been doing?"

"Aunt Marissa taught us," Cassie says.

"What did you think we were doing?" I ask.

"Not this," she says, and I laugh as she shoots my answer back at me. But there is something in her expression that alarms me. After all this time, does she not trust me? I have to be reading her wrong because the Rachel that has blossomed under my roof *does* trust me. Right?

"Seriously, Rachel, what did you think we were doing?"

She opens her mouth and closes it again. Her shoulders shrug. "Nothing, I guess."

"We need to talk," I say softly.

She nods. "You said that."

"Try them on," Cassie says.

Rachel sniffs, tugs on the mitts and holds her hands out. "They are perfect. They will keep me soooo warm. Thank you so much." She hugs Cassie and this time I'm the one fighting to keep my shit together.

"Let's eat," I say and Cassie climbs into the chair. Rachel takes a sip of her wine, but her hands are a bit shaky. Not only that, as Cassie fills us in on her day, and how Jacob shared his candy bar with her, Rachel picks at her food. Yeah, we definitely have to talk and this meal can't get over quick enough.

Cassie chats endlessly as we eat and once we're done, I take in the sauce all over her face. "Someone needs a bath," I say.

"I can do it," Rachel says.

"Nah, you go relax. It's your birthday celebration, and don't even think about doing the dishes."

She grimaces as she glances around the mess of the kitchen. "It looks like a hurricane tore through here."

I move close to her, as Cassie darts down the hall. "Leave it, Rach. Grab a glass of wine and go relax. Once I get Cassie bath and settled in bed, we need to talk."

"You said that already."

"I know."

I leave her in the kitchen and listen to her pour another glass of wine and make her way into the living room. The TV flicks on and I relax as I pour Cassie's bath, giving her extra bubbles.

"I love bubbles, Daddy."

"I know you do, kiddo."

"Daddy?"

Oh, boy. Cassie's using her serious voice which means this conversation is about to take a turn. "What is it?" I ask as I soak the wash cloth and take it to her face.

"How come Rachel can't be my mommy?"

How was that for a loaded question.

"You have a mommy," I say, but deep down, I want the same thing my daughter wants. I just hope after I tell Rachel how I feel, she'll want it all too.

"But I don't know my mommy. Grandma said she was coming back, but she didn't. Does mommy not like us, Daddy?"

"Mommy just had some things she needed to do."

"Gina has a mommy and daddy."

"I know she does."

"I want that, Daddy. I want a Mommy and a Daddy."

"I know you do, Cassie." I grab one of her water rubber duckies and toss it in, then I make an engine sound as I race it through the bubbles. Cassie laughs.

"That's not what a ducky sounds like," she explains, her mood changing.

"Why don't you show me then."

She takes the duck and as she quacks, the front door bell rings. I check my watch. Who the hell could that be?

"I'll get it," Rachel calls out.

I crane my neck to hear who is at the door. While I'm curious, I'm not about to leave Cassie in the tub my herself. I hear muffled voices, then Rachel's footsteps in the hall. Her eyes are wide, her skin pale when she enters the room.

I stand, my pulse jumping. "What's going on?" She points toward the front door, her gaze hesitant as she looks from me to Cassie back to me. "Rachel?"

"You...ah...you have company."

She doesn't need to say more for me to know who's at my door. I wipe my hand on the towel. "Would you mind getting Cassie out of the tub for me and take her to her room, please?"

"Okay."

As Rachel tends to Cassie, I take a deep, fueling breath and step into the hall. I take in the slim figure at my doorway, long blond hair that is now cut short, and features that have hardened over time.

"Sarah," I say as I close the distance. I look into her eyes, check her pupils.

"Hey Jay," she whispers quietly, seductively, going from one foot to the other as she looks past my shoulders, but no fucking way am I letting her near Cassie until I get some answers. "You look good."

I take in her sunken cheek bones, the way she's nervously licking her lips. "Have you been by to see your parents?"

"Not yet." She shuffles some more. "Can we talk?"

"I think that's a good idea, but it will have to wait until I get Cassie to bed."

Long lashes blink slowly over blue eyes. "Can I see her?"

"No," I say flatly, as anger wells up inside me. My first priority is keeping Cassie safe and well-adjusted. If she thinks I'm just going to spring her one my little girl, she's got another thing coming.

"I guess I screwed everything up," she says and gives a nervous laugh as she finger-combs her hair. That's when I notice the rings on her fingers.

I'm about to ask why the fuck she still has her wedding rings on, when Cassie calls out to me. "I'll be right there, kiddo," I say, and wave my hand for Sarah to take a seat in the living room. "I'll put Cassie to sleep, then we'll talk."

She nods and gingerly lowers herself onto the sofa. As she takes in the room, Cassie's toys on the floor, I hurry to my daughter, a million questions banging around my brain. Rachel has Cassie all tucked in, a book in her hand. She stands when I enter, her hands a bit shaky as she crosses her arm.

"Hey," she says. "I should go."

I grip my hair and tug. I don't want her to go. We need to talk, but I also have to talk to Sarah. We have a lifetime of things to figure out.

She makes a move to go around me and I touch her arm to stop her. "I didn't know she was going to show up, Rachel."

"I know."

"I'm sorry about this." She sniffs and averts my gaze. "Let me get things straightened out here, then I'll call you, okay? We need to talk."

"Okay," she says, and turns to Cassie. "Bye, Cassie," she says and disappears out the door.

Bye, Cassie.

Jesus fucking Christ, why would she say it like that—like she's leaving here—us—for good.

17

RACHEL

Numb.

That's the only word I can use to describe what I'm feeling as I rush down the hall and out of Jaxon's house, once and for all. In my haste, I fail to grab the mittens they made me, but maybe it's better that I leave them behind. Wearing them would be a constant reminder of what I can't have.

I try to sort things through, my thoughts still forming within the scrambling haze. One thing is for certain, I believe Jaxon had no idea his 'wife' was going to show up. There was a genuine honesty in his eyes, those concerned worry lines running long and deep, mirrored truth. But after I saw the wedding rings, my insecurities, threads from the past, cast doubts. Those rings threatened me, displaced me, told me Sarah was home to get her life and family back, and I would never have the chance to be in any of Cassie's classroom pictures.

From the heated look in Sarah's eyes, it was clear she was looking for a debate, one that said she belonged and I didn't.

Her expression held a challenge. Battle lines were being drawn in the sand. Instead of giving her what she wanted, I hid in the bathroom with Cassie while Jaxon and his wife faced off.

Tears fall and I fight the weight on my shoulders as I hike my backpack up and let myself into my sorority house—my real world. The girls call out to me from the kitchen, but I ignore them as I rush through the house. With dejection punching me in the chest, I'm in no state of mind to deal with their questions. I need to get to my room, get myself together. My eyes blur with tears as I take the stairs two at a time.

Jaxon is still married.

Fresh grief rides through my veins, flooding my body with turbulence and my legs threaten to give out. My damn heart pounds against my ribcage as I fish my bedroom key from my bag, but when I see a box sitting outside my door, I go still. Sylvie comes up the stairs, her footsteps slow and steady, and I wipe my face with the back of my hand. I don't want her to see me crying. I don't want to answer questions, or admit that I'd been a fool. Jaxon and I had been playing house. Nothing else.

"Hey Rachel, you okay?"

I unlock my door, and pick up the box. Trying my best to act casual, and pretend that my heart hasn't been shred to pieces—with a cheese grader. "How long has this been here?"

"A week I think."

I keep my back to Sylvie and check the big box for a return address. "Who is it from?"

"I don't know. Some old dude dressed in a suit delivered it here."

What the hell? "It didn't come from a courier?"

"No, he was driving a Buick or something. Why, what's is it?"

"Did he say who this was from?"

"Didn't ask." I turn to her, and she takes a step toward me. "Jesus, Rachel, what's going on? Are you okay, you look like you've been crying?"

"I'm fine," I lie and hurry inside my room, shutting the door tightly behind me.

I drop the box on my bed and go to my window. I look across to Jaxon's house but his bedroom is dark. Sarah's car is still sitting in the driveway.

Jaxon is still married.

Nausea wells up inside me to think all this time Jaxon has been married. But I should have known, right? He said she took off without looking back. How could I ever have thought they'd gotten a divorce? God, I am so much like those women my father used to whore around with. Cassie is going to hate me as much as I hated them.

I swallow, my throat so tight, it's almost impossible to breathe.

An anxious ball lodges in my gut as another thought hits. Is this what Jaxon wanted to talk to me about? That once Sarah returned home, they'd be getting back together—because they were still married? He kept talking about timing. He might not have known she'd show up at his door, but did he know she was home, and that they would be getting the tree tomorrow? Was that why he wanted to cele-brate my birthday early? So I could be gone before Sarah moved back in, and they could go tree hunting as a family. A real one. Not the one I was pretending was mine.

He was never yours.

As anxiety threatens to overwhelm me, I close my eyes and take a few deep breaths. That's when my thoughts take a resounding halt, and slowly begins to back up, change paths— a train reversing the engine with a screech roar and hopping on to another rail.

As I consider everything we've been through, from our first meeting to the knitting, baking my favorite cookies, making my favorite meal, my convictions waver. I think back to the man Jaxon is. A great father, lover, friend. A man with more integrity in his pinky than my father...my ex.

Jaxon is a good man.

As I reflect on that, I glance around the room, my eyes refocusing, losing the blurry haze. Up until tonight, things had been so good between us. Has it really changed, or is it just past experiences coloring my view? My heart leaps, and tendrils of hope seep through my veins, pushing back all negative thoughts, refusing to let me think the worst of him.

The truth is, would a man pining for his 'wife', a man I'm in love with, touch me with such tender care, drive me to school every day to ensure I'm warm and safe? His actions speak volumes of his character—show the real man behind the tough exterior. I think about that for a fleeting second, which stretches, expands, fills my thoughts with positive things, like how he took me to meet his friends. Would he do that if this was sex only, if he weren't falling for me the same way I was falling for him?

My heart beats harder, racing into my throat. Maybe tonight's talk wasn't about letting me down easily, and more about celebrating my birthday early, and opening up about how we felt, so we could all go pick out a tree as a family. A rush of optimism slams through me.

I think back to what he once said about Sarah. She has a way of saying things to get what she wants. Was that why she flashed her ring? She came back home after she found out about me, which makes me think of that old saying: She might not want him, but she doesn't want anyone else to have him. Was this the case with her? She had no worries about Jaxon until her friend said he was with me. I take a long time to mull that over and while it's so easy to let past mistakes influence me, doubt leaves my brain. A new kind of anxiety takes hold, one that is yelling at me to go back over there and stand united with the man I love. I need to let him know I'm with him for the good times and the bad.

My phone pings and my heart soars when I see a text from the man occupying my thoughts.

Rach, I'm sorry.

Wait, what? He's sorry? What is he sorry for? Even after my epiphany, old worries creep back in.

I didn't know she was back, or that she'd show up here out of the blue.

I relax, all the love I feel for the hot daddy next door flooding me.

I know.

Why did you leave?

I want to go over there more than anything, I really do. But I'm an adult, confident in my feelings for the man next door, and confident in his for me, so I text back. *To give you two time to talk.*

Yeah, I guess we need to.

Is she still there?

In the bathroom. We have a lot to talk about.

I understand.

You and I do, too. Come home after Sarah leaves, okay. I don't care what time it is. I'll be waiting up for you. I need to see you, Rach.

My heat swells. Sara's not staying and he needs to see me.

I type in *I love you*, take a deep breath, then delete it. I don't want the first time he hears that from me to be through text. I change the text to, *Okay.*

I read his text again and then close my eyes, pressing my phone to my chest as if it will bring Jaxon closer to me. Warmth seeps through me and pushes the chill of anxiety away. I open my eyes again and see the box on my bed. I had totally forgotten about it in my angst over Sara.

I toss my phone onto my nightstand and tear into the box. But as soon as I see the contents, I know Jaxon will never, ever in this lifetime, hear those three little words, *I love you*, from me.

JAXON

Jaxon

"Hey Cassie, why don't you open that one there," I say and point to the big box under the Christmas tree. It's taking everything inside me to keep a smile on my face, and make sure my daughter has the perfect Christmas morning.

"What is it, Daddy?" she asks her face beaming, but underneath our smiles we're both hurting. After Rachel left us seventeen days ago, went back to her place, we never set eyes on her again. I thought she was going to come over after Sarah and I had a talk, but when I texted her and didn't get an answer, I checked the driveway to find her car gone. I went over, and asked her roommates where she'd gone, only to be told she'd received a big package and then upped and left.

Who was the package from and where the fuck did she go?

Did she think Sarah and I were getting back together? I'd gotten the sense that she knew different, which has left me wracking my brain to figure this shit out.

You weren't enough for her, Jaxon.

Fuck man, could that have been it? Could she have cut out of here because she was done with us and didn't know how to tell us. I'm driving myself crazy trying to figure this out, and why the hell isn't she answering any of my texts?

"Daddy, it's a dolly," Cassie says and I blink to get myself back in the present. But my daughter is a smart one. She sets the doll down, comes over to me and puts her hands on my cheek. "Daddy, do you miss Rachel?"

How the hell do I answer that?

I swallow, wanting to lie for her sake, but I swore I'd always to be honest with my child—with everyone. "Yeah, kiddo, I do."

"I do too." Her hands fall from my face. "When is she coming back?"

"I'm not sure."

She looks down, so goddamn sad, my already broken heart cracks a little more. I never thought Rachel would up and leave like Sarah did. I'm angry about that, angry that she would hurt Cassie. Hurt me.

"I'm glad she's not my mommy," she says and it takes everything in me not to fucking sob.

"Hey why don't you see what's in that package. It's a special one from me."

As I distract Cassie, a knock comes on my door and my heart leaps with hope. "You open that and I'll be right back." I push off the couch I hurry to the door, but when I open it, it's Judy and Karl on my stoop. I catch the worried look on their faces and exhale a sharps breath.

"What's going on?" I ask.

"Have you seen Sarah?" Judy asks, and toys with the pearls around her neck—a nervous tick. "Is she here?"

"No," I say. After that first night, I refused to let Sarah back in my home until she could prove she was clean and sober for the next few months. I had to make sure she was on the straight and narrow before I let her see Cassie. She had to prove herself to us.

"She left last night, said she was coming here," Karl informs me.

I shake my head. Here we fucking go again. "She's not here."

"Who is Cassie talking to?" Judy asks. What, does she think I'm fucking lying to her?

"It's a new interactive game I got her for Christmas."

Judy makes a face, like she'd just sucked on something sour. "Oh, I thought it was that *girl*."

I crack my neck, bite back a sharp response. "That girl, as in Rachel?"

"Yes."

"We haven't seen her since Sarah's been back," I say

"It's for the best." Judy leans in and almost hisses, "She's trouble, Jaxon."

Her insulting works get my back up. On the defense, I ask. "What make you say that?"

I don't miss the nervous glance Judy casts Karl's way, or the way Karl is tugging on his collar like his shirt just shrank two sizes.

What the fuck have they done?

"What?" I ask through clenched teeth, my fingers clenching and unclenching at my side.

"Well, Karl took it upon himself to check into her background. You never can be too sure about anyone these days."

Motherfucker.

I pinch the bridge of my nose and try to keep my shit together. "What did you do?"

"Karl hired a private detective. He's been following Rachel, and dug up information on her. He even paid a visit to her old boyfriend in New York. The man was charged with assault, you know. Not the kind of people we want in Cassie's life, Jaxon."

For one brief second I'm frozen with shock, my words lodged into my throat. Cassie's voice in the background pulls me back. "Oh, my fuck, no. You didn't. Tell me you didn't," I say my voice rising, bordering on panic.

"This ex said he'd been trying to find Rachel. To return her belongings," Karl explain, oblivious to what he's done, the danger he put Rachel in.

I grip the doorframe as rage prowls through me. "Tell me your detective wasn't stupid enough to give an address."

"No, no of course not," Judy says waving a dismissive hand. "He said he'd deliver them to her himself."

Fear trickles down my spine. "What did he deliver?"

"I don't know. A box of something I guess."

The box.

Jesus, fuck.

An all-consuming need to bolt from my house and find Rachel pulls at me. I try to calm myself. I can't think clearly when I'm upset. "When did this happen?"

"What does it matter?"

"It matters, okay," I practically shout.

"He went to New York before Sarah came home. Why are you so upset? None of this matters now."

Panic curls through my blood. "Oh, it matters."

"Sarah is home and Cassie has her rightful mother back."

"Then where is she, Judy?" I bluntly ask, my voice far colder than it was moments ago. "Where is her mother on Christmas morning?"

"I...don't know."

"Two things," I say, a new desperation racing through me. "Look closely at your own daughter before you decide what kind of people you want in Cassie's life, and two, I want every piece of information that investigator has on Rachel."

RACHEL

From my grandmother's old homestead in upstate Pennsylvania, I glance out the back window and watch the snow blanket the yard. It's a gorgeous Christmas afternoon, the kind I remember from when I was very young, yet there is no happiness, no sense of excitement for me today. In fact, my heart aches with the opposite of happiness. I hug myself against the cool winter draft coming in through the old windowpane and exhale a heavy sign.

Grandma is having her afternoon tea and scones in the kitchen, but I haven't been able to eat much since running away from my sorority a couple weeks ago—from Jaxon and Cassie. I have a million texts on my phone, but they've been coming in less and less. I guess Jaxon has finally realized I wasn't going to answer and had given up.

A hiccupping sob catching in my throat.

"Something wrong?" Grandma asks from the other room, and I swallow down the pain, and try to inject a lightness in my voice that I don't feel.

"Everything is fine, Grandma," I fib, sure nothing will ever be fine again. But I've been pretty much fibbing since I arrived, not that Grandma can't see right through me. She might be old, but she's astute, and has lived long enough to know when someone is suffering.

Still though, I'm not about to lay my sob story on an elderly woman I've never really been close to. There is nothing she can do about my predicament, anyway. Predicament? Is that what I'm calling it now?

I think everything through, from the second I exchanged words with Jaxon, until I found that box left outside my bedroom door—a box with a few of my old belongings—Dylan's way of sending a message that he knows where I am and can get to me at any time. It took all of three seconds to realize the danger, and ten more minutes for me to gather a few things, jump in my car and find temporary shelter and refuge at my grandmother's place. No one, not even Jaxon knows about the old homestead.

My heart pounds at that, a new kind of fear creeping its way along my veins as I peer outside, look for signs of the man who had that box delivered to my house. My God, if he ever found out I was with Jaxon, if he ever used Cassie as a threat, I just…Jesus, I can't let my thoughts go to such a dark and scary place. But if something did happen, and Jaxon ever got his hands on Dylan, he'd tear him into two pieces. He'd end up in prison and would undoubtedly lose his daughter for good. No way could I hang around and let any of those scenarios play out. Leaving was my only choice, otherwise…

Another sound crawls out of my throat, and I step away from the window. I shake my head to clear it and pad through the old house. That old fake tree from my childhood sits propped up in the corner, the blinking lights no longer working. Not much has changed since I used to visit here with my folks. Grandma might have mellowed a bit when talking about my mother, become a bit less judgmental of her. But now that she's gone, it's too little too late. She even seems a little sympathetic toward me, and the fact that I fled home at eighteen because of my father. Speaking of my father, my grandmother hasn't heard from him in years, and I kind of think that's a little sad, considering she was the only one who stood by his side, justified his disgusting behavior.

Parents see things the way they want to see them, I guess. Look at Sarah's folks. They clearly want Sarah back, and back in her daughter's life, despite all the pain she brought everyone. But how dare they blame Jaxon for her leaving in the first place? He's a good man, the best man I know.

Stop thinking about him, Rachel.

Truthfully, I have no idea where I go from here. At least I have the Christmas break to figure it out. Right now, though, I'm thinking I'll move into a new place near Penn State to finish my degree, but make sure it's far enough from Jaxon that I never have to set eyes on him again—bring any kind of danger into his life. I have to take Dylan's threat seriously, and from here on out, I'll keep my head down, and stay off anyone's radar.

"You were on mine the second you moved in next door."

As Jaxon's words ping through my brain, I clench down on my jaw hard enough to cause the muscle to throb. Maybe I need to try some type of pain therapy to forget him. Maybe I'll look into purchasing a Taser and use it on myself. I give a humorless laugh as I step into the kitchen. With the oven on and a pot boiling on the stovetop, it's much warmer than the other areas of the house. Yellowing daisy wallpaper covering the walls, and peeling around the edges brings back thoughts of my mother. She loved daisies. I sniff, but when I catch the worry in grandma's eyes, I turn from her.

Christmas should be filled with joy, laugher and loved ones, and I don't want to bring Grandma down into my pit of despair. She hands me a glass of tea, even though I hadn't asked for one. In the two weeks I've been here, I've lost all the weight I put on thanks to Jaxon making my lunches and sharing our meals.

"The turkey is in the oven," Grandma says with a smile on her face that doesn't quite reach her eyes. "Mabel and Gracie are bringing the fixings. We'll all have a big Christmas meal," she says and pats my hands slightly. "It will be fun."

I force a smile, take in the lines around her eyes, the tight gray curls pinching her scalp. There is a sadness about her, too. She can try to hide it from me, but underneath the façade, Grandma has regrets. Of that I'm certain.

"Thanks for letting me share the holidays with you," I say.

"You're always welcome here, Rachel."

I take a sip of tea and glance around the kitchen. "Is there anything I can do to help?"

"If you want to get some wood from the shed that would help," she says. I nod and set my tea down. There's plenty of wood in the rack by the fireplace, but I get that she's just trying to give me chores to take my mind off things, even though she has no idea what those things are.

I walk to the front door, pull on my boots and coat, and grab my dollar store mittens and hat from the bench. But as soon as I close my fingers around them, my thoughts go to Jaxon and Cassie and the mitts they knitted for my birthday. Tears well up in my eyes. I still can't believe they did that. No one has ever done anything so thoughtful or touching. Those mitts mean the world to me and I wish I had grabbed them before I fled. Just a little something tangible to hold on to, a little memory to pack away and take out when my heart isn't quite so broken, although I'm not sure that time will ever come. Jaxon is the sweetest man I've ever met, and his daughter has my heart. To think he went through such an effort for me. My chest nearly burst with the love I feel for him.

I tug the hat on and hold my mitts in one had as I open

the door with the other. But when I come face to face with a very familiar man, his hand raised to knock, the mittens slip from my fingers and I falter backward.

No!

No. No. No. This can't be happening.

"What? How?" I begin, fear crawling up from the depths of my stomach. I glance past his shoulders, see the running vehicle in the driveway. This can't be happening. I blink, open my eyes again, but he's still there. The room spins around me, and breathing becomes a little more difficult.

How did he find me?

"What...what are you doing here?" I ask around a tongue gone thick.

"Rachel..." As my legs go out from underneath me, the most warm, caring hands I ever had the pleasure of touching me capture me before I fall.

"Jaxon," I say, his name catching in my throat.

He holds my trembling body to his, and through our winter coats, his heart pounds hard against my chest. Unable to help myself, I breathe him in, and hold his scent in my lungs never wanting to forget it. Strong hands grip me tighter, and as big fingers fist my hair and his aroma plumes through my blood, I cry. I cry hard. I cry for my mother, my father, for Jaxon and Cassie. I cry for love and loss...years of pain.

"Hey," he whispers, and holds me tight until I finally stop trembling.

"Jaxon, you...you can't be here," I whisper, and pound against his chest. "You have to go."

He inches back, and I nearly sob again when I catch the pain, the fearful confusion, bracketing his blue eyes. I hurt him. Deeply. But what choice did I have? It was the only way I could protect him and his daughter.

"I'll go, Rachel. But you're coming with me," he says, and I glance at his running car again, catch sight of Cassie in the back seat. Her worried blue eyes, big and afraid, much like her father's, latch onto mine.

My knees let go, and I break from the circle of Jaxon's arms. Leaning forward, I place my hand on my stomach, to fight back the nausea. I added to that little's girl's loss, her pain. I hate myself for that, especially since all I ever wanted to do was love her. I breathe through the hurt, the bile punching into my throat.

"Rachel—" Jaxon begins.

"No," I blurt out, hating myself, hating this entire situation, I step farther away from Jaxon. Being with me is unsafe. I have to make him understand that.

"Is everything okay, dear?" Grandmas asks from the kitchen doorway.

"Everything is fine, Grandma."

She hesitates for a moment. "I'll be in the kitchen if you need me."

I swallow painfully. "How..."

"Judy and Karl had a private investigator look into your past," he announces, coming right to the point.

My vision clouds as a million questions race through my mind. I stumble again, and back up until my knees hit the sofa. The wind whips through the house, but Jaxon doesn't close the front door, not with his daughter still inside a running car.

"Why...why would they do that?"

Jaxon glances over his shoulder to check on his daughter, then takes a measured step toward me. Instead of answering, he says, "At first, I thought you left because of Sarah. I saw the rings on her finger and can only assume she flashed them at you, too. I once told you she has a knack for making people believe what they want."

"She did flash them," I say, my voice as shaky as my body. I need him to go but I can't let him think I never believed he was one of the good guys. "At first I thought you were still married, Jaxon. When we were...well you know. I didn't give it much thought. I guess we were busy doing other things." I brush my hair from my face, and grab a tissue from the box on the coffee table. I dab my eyes and then pluck at the ends. "Then she flashed her rings, made it clear I needed to go. I wasn't going to at first, but those diamonds jump-started my brain and I couldn't figure out how you could have gotten a divorce when you said she left suddenly and never looked back. I hated myself for being..." I stop to do air quotes around the words, "'the other woman.'" I was no better than those women..."

He fists his hair and tugs. "Your father, I know."

I look down at the torn tissue, and keep ripping at it. "I couldn't stand the idea of Cassie hating me the way I hated all those women, but the more I thought about it, the more I reasoned it out. You'd never purposely hurt me or use me, Jaxon. You're a kind man with integrity. More integrity in that baby finger than any other man I know. So, I realized that even though you might not have had the papers to prove you two were over, the marriage was over in your head and in your heart."

"It's also over on paper."

My head jerks back up. "It is?"

"I had an investigator find her and serve her papers. She didn't show up to court and the judge awarded the divorce based on the facts shown on my petition. Sarah still wore the rings. I guess she never thought I'd go through with it."

"Where is she now?" I ask, not sure if I want to really know.

He shrugs, and shakes his head, disgust written all over his face. "Who knows. Gone again, I guess."

Oh, his poor daughter. "Cassie..." I croak out.

"She never got to meet her. I told her she had to prove

she was clean and had her act together before I let her into Cassie's life."

"I'm so sorry, Jaxon. I know how much you wanted Cassie to have a mother."

"Not a mother that we we're not enough for, Rach," he says, his voice lower, softer.

"Of course not."

"Once I realized you knew better than to think I was still married and going to fall back into a life with Sarah, I couldn't help but think you left because we weren't enough either." He shrugs again. "Past experiences and all."

"I understand, Jaxon. We all have our demons but it's not like that," I say quickly. I can't let him think that. Any woman in her right mind would be crazy to leave him and his daughter. I only left to protect them, because my ex wasn't in his right mind.

"I know."

I let out a breath, relieved at that.

He takes one more step toward me, captures my hand in his and lifts until I'm standing on wobbly legs. But I don't have to worry about falling. He secures one arm around my waist, and places a comforting hand on my cheek.

"I was lost and confused for weeks, Rachel, and had no idea where you were, or why you left until Judy and Karl showed up at my door. That's when everything fell into place for me."

"You know, then," I blurt out. "You know Dylan found me."

"He never found you, and for his sake, he'd better not ever try." His nostrils flare, the blue of his eyes sharpening. "As a matter of fact, maybe Jericho and the rest of the guys will go with me and pay him a visit. Give him a chance to pick on someone his own size."

My pulse leaps, and blood rushes to my brain. "No, Jaxon.

That's one of the reasons why I left. I can't let you go down that road. Getting into trouble, fighting…" I pound on his chest again. "You're not safe when you're with me. If Dylan ever threatened you…Cassie. Oh, God," I cry out. "You have to think about what's best for Cassie."

"I am, that's why I said I wasn't leaving here without you. Dylan doesn't know where you are. You left to protect us, not because you thought I was or that we weren't enough, and I love you for that, Rachel, I really do."

"You…love me for that."

"Let me say this again. I love you, Rachel. That's what I wanted to talk to you about the night you ran away on us. I love you and want you in our lives. I want you in Cassie's life. I'm careful who I bring in to Cassie's life. At first I was worried about bringing you in,. I knew you were on the run, Rach, but you never have to run again. You're the only person good enough for my daughter, and rest assured no one is ever going to hurt you again."

"Jaxon, it's…I'm afraid. Dylan…"

"He doesn't know where you are, and besides, once you move in with us and change your last name, his chances drop from slim to none."

I angle my head, sort through is words. "Why would I change my last name?"

"I'd really like you to take on mine when we get married, but I get it women don't always do that today, so if you don't want to—"

What?

Married?

"What are you saying?" I ask, my heart racing like a hamster on a wheel.

He drops to one knee, and my breath leaves my lungs in a whoosh.

"Will you marry me, Rachel. Will you be my wife, Cassie's

mother?"

Tears fall again, harder this time, soaking the front of my coat. I sink to my knees with him and he brushes my hair back. "I love you, Rachel. And there is a little girl in that car that loves you, too. Say yes, and I'll go get her."

I pause as tears run down my eyes. My heart is pounding so hard in my ears, I'm not sure I'm hearing things right.

"Rach?"

"Say yes, child," Grandma says from the kitchen.

A big hiccupping laugh—or cry, I can't be sure—climbs out of my throat. "Yes, Jaxon. Yes, a million times over."

Worry leaves his eyes and he displays those sexy dimples as he smiles at me and presses his lips to mine. "I love you."

"I love you, too."

He stands, and pulls me up with him. He guides me to the sofa and I sit. "Don't move." He gives me a warning glare.

"I won't," I say through a garbled chuckle.

Jaxon dashes out the door, and comes back in with Cassie. She's carrying a picnic basket in one hand, a doll in the other.

"Rachel," she squeals, dropping both and running toward me. I give her a big hug, and she starts talking about a kite, and a picnic, and my birthday.

"Slow down, kiddo," I say, and Jaxon drops grabs the picnic basket, and drops his knees in front of us. "What's going on?" I ask.

He takes one of my hand in his. "Do you remember what you told me you wanted for your birthday?"

"Yes, another day with my mother."

"We couldn't make that happen, but we wanted to try our best. We had plans to get our Christmas tree on your birthday, then take you to the park, fly a kite, have a picnic. All the things you did with your mother. But you left before we could do any of that."

"Ohmigod, Jaxon," I say and place my free hand over my

face as my heart fills will all the love I have for him and his daughter.

"The food didn't make it, but there are a few things in that basket that we still want to give you."

"Now, Daddy?" Cassie asks.

"Now, kiddo," he says.

I swipe my tears away and Cassie reaches into the basket. I laugh when she pulls out those gummy green leaves I like.

"You remembered," I say, barely able to speak.

"I remembered," he says softly as he places his hand on my cheek.

Cassie reaches in and what she pulls out next has the tears falling again. "Jaxon," I blubber as I take the picture from Cassie. "How?"

"I know a guy who knows a guy and he was able to digitally restore it. Cassie picked the frame out."

I look from the picture of my mom and me, the one that was ruined that night that freshman attacked me, and take in the sweet girl beaming up at me. Jaxon came to my rescue that night, and in my heart, I know as long as I'm with him, no one will ever hurt me again.

"It's perfect, Cassie. Thank you." I grab another tissue, wipe my face and reach for both Jaxon's and Cassie's hands. "I have a confession."

Jaxon stiffens, the worry lines bracketing his eyes deepening. "What?"

"I did want another day with my mother for my birthday, but I secretly wished for something else."

Jaxon looks from me, to his rather quiet daughter, back to me. "Anything. You name it, it's yours."

"What I wished for was a lifetime with you."

Jaxon's features soften as he leans in, and gently puts his lips on mine. Our first display of affection in front of Cassie.

"Daddy!" Cassie exclaims.

We both laugh and Jaxon rubs his daughter's head. "Get used to it, Cassie. Rachel is coming to live with us and she's going to be your new mommy. I know you were just angry and upset this morning when you said you didn't want that."

Her big blue eyes fill with tears as she throws her arms around me. "I want you to be my mommy," she says. "I was just sad when I said that."

"I want to be your mommy, Cassie. And I'm sorry I made you sad. I never wanted to make you sad. Do you forgive me?"

"I forgive you," she says, then glances at her daddy. She crinkles her nose and we both know she's about to say something profound. "But do I call you mommy?"

"That depends—" Jaxon begins.

"Do you want to, Cassie?" I ask. She nods her head, her ponytail bouncing. "Good," I say. "After your daddy and I get married, I can officially adopt you, and I'll be your mommy."

As Cassie hugs me again, Jaxon mouths the words, "Thank you."

Grandma clears her throat from the kitchen, and I put my hands on Cassie's shoulders. "There is someone I want you to meet."

"Who?"

"Your new grandmother."

Her eyes open wide. "I get another grandmother?"

Jaxon and I laugh. "Well actually, she's my grandmother which makes her your great-grandmother."

"I...I don't understand. Do I call her Grandma?"

"Yes, child, you call me Grandma." I glance up to see my grandmother holding her arms out to Cassie. "Why don't you come here and say hello."

Jaxon gives Cassie a nod and she leaves my arms and goes to her new great-grandmother.

"Aren't you a pretty one." Grandma looks from Cassie to Jaxon and me. She touches Cassie's ponytail, and I know the two are going to hit it off. She might not have been the best grandmother to me, but she's mellowed over the years, has lots of regrets and I know damn well she's going to fix all her mistakes with this sweet little girl. Cassie has been a gift to all of us.

Cassie curls her ponytail through her fingers. "Daddy gives me Nightmare Moon, but Rachel." She stops and corrects herself, like the precocious little girl she is. "I mean my new mommy gives me Twisted Pony." I stare at Cassie and feel like I've come full circle, and that circle is now bubbling with love.

Grandma laughs and says, "How would you like to help me make a pie? We're having a big turkey dinner. I hope you can stay."

I nod, and Cassie excitedly dashes in to the kitchen. Grandma winks at me and follows Cassie, giving Jaxon and me a few minutes alone.

"I have a confession, too," he says and pulls me to him.

"Oh?" I snuggle against him, and slide my arms around his back.

"I fell in love with the sorority girl next door, and I still don't know her last name."

I give a casual shrug. "Does it even matter now?"

He cocks his head. "Why wouldn't it matter?"

"Because as fast as I can, I want to change it to your last name."

"Really?"

"Yeah, really."

He picks me up and spins me. "You've made me the happiest man in the world. I really like the sound of Rachel Morgan, but you don't have to—"

"Jaxon."

"Yeah?"

"Shut up and kiss the future Rachel Morgan already."

THANK YOU!

Thank you so much for reading, **Single Dad Next Door.** I hope you enjoyed the story as much as I loved writing it. Be sure to read on for an excerpt of **Confessions of a Bad Boy Cop.**

Interested in leaving a review? Please do! Reviews help readers connect with books that work for them. I appreciate all reviews, whether positive or negative.

Happy Reading,
Cathryn

CONFESSIONS OF A BAD BOY COP

LAYLA

S ix years ago:

Dad's pool party is in full swing by the time I step into the backyard, in search of free alcohol for myself—and my friends, who are eagerly waiting inside. Hey, why shouldn't I sneak a few bottles, right? It's summer vacation. I just worked an insane double shift at the mall food court, and I wouldn't mind a cold drink to wind down after a long-ass day with no breaks because my co-worker called in sick. Sick, my ass. I heard she hooked up with a couple guys and went to the beach.

Scorching sunshine beats down on me as I glance around the deck, which is dotted with loud, obnoxious people. I take in the hedonistic atmosphere and skimpy bathing suits as stiff drinks are downed in record time. I shake my head in disgust. Sometimes I feel like I'm the only adult in the house. Yes, I know Mom and Dad had me when they were too young, lost great scholarships because of it—something my mother always likes to point out—but still, they're supposed to be the grown ups in this relationship, yet again and again, they prove they're not.

I search out my mom, and my heart squeezes when I find her sitting on the edge of the pool. Cheeks pink from the sun, not to mention too much alcohol, she looks lost in thought as she runs a hand through her wet hair, and kicks her legs in the water. I grab the lotion and head straight for her.

I go down on my knees. "Mom," I say, and touch her shoulder gently, not wanting to alarm her. "You might want to get out of the sun."

She waves her hand at me like I'm nothing but a nuisance fly. "What are you doing here?"

My heart sinks into my stomach at her dismissive, angry tone. "I just got home from work." I hand her the lotion and she glares at it like I've just given her a store-bought enema kit.

"If you want to make yourself useful, grab me another drink." She shakes her glass at me, and the melting ice clicks on the bottom. As the sound grates on my last nerve, I want to tell her she's had enough, but it will only lead to a fight. I take the glass and shut my mouth, making a mental note to leave Tylenol and water by her bed the way I always do when she's on a bender, which is pretty much every weekend, and then some.

As I make my way to the outdoor bar, I let my gaze rake over the crowd a second time. Most of the male cops Dad work with are either falling over themselves drunk, or hitting on someone else's wife.

Pigs.

Every last one of them.

Well except for Jack Michaels, Dad's partner and best

friend. I've known Jack forever and have yet to see him get out of control like the others. In fact, he's always rigid, reserved, scanning the room for trouble. A predator in search of his prey. God, I want to be the deer in his headlights. A fine shiver moves through my body, hitting every hot button along the way to the needy spot between my legs. Yeah, that's right. I have it bad for my Dad's best friend.

I pour my mom's drink, making it extra watery, and set it on the bar top. I bend, and Jack's gaze lands on me the second I snatch a couple of coolers from the bucket, and casually slide them into my backpack. I give him a small grin, and put the bag over my shoulder—a dare of sorts. He pushes off the table he'd been leaning against and folds big arms over a broad chest—a *bare* broad chest that my fingers itch to explore—his piercing gaze stealing the breath from my lungs.

Jeez, he is so freaking good looking, so rough around the edges, it makes me all jittery inside. He's taller than every other guy at the precinct, and has an athletic, rock-hard body that any criminal would be a fool to challenge. But I want to challenge him. Oh yeah, just once I want to push him until he loses that hard-earned control and acts on the heat between us. The sexual tension is off the charts, so powerful and volatile I can't believe the other *adults* can't feel it. Then again, maybe they can. Maybe they all know how we feel about each other, but don't much care because Jack is a good man, and a good cop, who wouldn't do anything illegal.

But I won't always be seventeen.

My body warms as his gaze rakes over me, his brilliant blue eyes holding me in place, keeping me captive. I stare back, and hold my own against him like I always do as he closes the distance between us. He stands over me, crowds me, and I toy with the button on my blouse, another little thing I do to tease him. I know it works because his gaze drops to my fingers, the muscles along his jaw rippling as he clenches his teeth hard. He dips his head, his mouth so close to mine, it's all I can do not to go up on my toes and press my lips to his. Instead, I swipe my tongue over my bottom lip, leaving a streak of moisture that invites him in for a taste.

"Do you know what you're doing?" he asks.

Poking the bear?

Then again, maybe he's talking about the alcohol, and not my sexual teasing. But I can't help myself around him. From the second I hit puberty a few years ago, I've wanted Jack in my arms and in my bed. I can't tell you how many nights I've laid between the sheets, running my hands over my body, and pretending they were his. There's sixteen years difference between us, but I'm a minor until next month, so those years might as well be a chasm. As soon as I turn eighteen and move into my dorm room at University of Texas at San Antonio—a college close to home so I can keep an eye on my mom—I don't think the gap will come into play at all. Then again, this is Dad's best friend, and if I want him in my bed, I'm going to have to do more than play with the button on my shirt.

"It's just a couple of coolers," I say to him. "My friends and I are going to sip them and watch a movie inside."

His nostrils flare and his gaze drops to my mouth again, fixates on it. "You're too young to drink."

"Are you going to tell on me?" I ask, and coil my hair around my finger, playing the innocent. The truth is I *am* innocent. Sure, I've made out with guys, but I'm saving myself for Jack. Not that it's hard to say no to the fumbling idiots my age. But for my first time, I want a real man to take me. A man who knows his way around a woman's body, not some stupid jock who hits the finish line a second after the gun goes off.

I don't know this firsthand, of course, but my best friend Luanne isn't saving herself for anyone. She sleeps with a different guy every weekend and is well aware of my obsession with Jack. While she thinks I should get a few fucks under my belt so I'll know how to please a guy like him once I finally get him into my bed, I disagree. I want him to be my first, and I have a feeling that once I give him my virginity, it will bring us closer, and keep us together.

Patience...that's all I need.

"I'm no snitch," he says.

"I never thought you were, but if you're so worried about me having a few drinks, maybe you'd like to discipline me yourself."

"Layla..." he murmurs, his jaw doing that clenching and unclenching thing again.

"I suppose you could always put me over your knee and give me a good hard spanking for my disobedience."

"Fuck," he murmurs, and ignoring his *no touch rule*, his hand moves, his knuckles brushing against mine and sending heat straight to my sex. It moistens and clenches, aching for his attention, something hard to grip on to. His big, broad frame is blocking mine and no one can see us. I step closer, push my body against his and feel his huge cock swelling in his swim trunks.

It thrills me and urges me on. I move against him and he puts his hands on my shoulders to stop me. "We can't," he says through gritted teeth. "We've been over this."

"I know," I say. "But when we can, it's going to be amazing."

"Layla," he grumbles and steps back from me. The bottles in my backpack clink and he looks over his shoulder, then back at me. "No driving?"

"Of course not."

"You know alcohol impairs—"

"Jack," I begin and put my hand on his chest. He sucks in a sharp breath, and every muscle in his body goes rigid as I splay my fingers. I resist the urge to glance down, to see that other muscle that always grows hard from my touch.

"No touching," he says, but his voice belies his actions as he takes as small step toward me, giving me better access to his body.

I keep my palm on his body and say, "Don't you trust me?"

"I don't trust the guys you're hanging with, Layla," he says and looks over my head.

"Liam and Caleb?" I shrug and wave a dismissive hand. "Those guys are innocent."

Jack dips his head again, and scoffs. "Are you forgetting I was once a seventeen year old boy? I don't want you to find yourself in a situation that you can't get out of."

"That's not going to happen as long as I have you watching over me." I smile sweetly and say, "Now is it, Jack?"

"What about when I'm not watching?" he asks.

I swipe my tongue over my bottom lip again and remove my hand from his chest. I instantly miss his warmth, but console myself with the fact that someday we'll be together and can touch each other at whim.

"But you're always watching, Jack." I hand him mom's drink to deliver, and spin around. I give an extra shake to my backside as I saunter into the house. I shut the patio door behind me, but I feel his eyes on me, burning through my clothes and caressing my naked body.

"Did you get it?" Caleb asks and practically rips my backpack from my shoulder.

"I grabbed a few coolers."

Liam unravels himself from Luanne and rushes toward us to help Caleb tear through the backpack. "Come on, man. What about the harder stuff?" he asks.

"I couldn't." I shrug innocently. "One of my Dad's friends caught me. I'm lucky I got away with the few bottles I was able to snag. For a minute there I thought he was going to put me over his knee and spank me." I slide my gaze to Luanne, and she grins, knowing exactly who I'm talking about, and just how much I'd love to be put over his knee and disciplined.

"Fucking girly drinks," Caleb says as he pulls the vodka coolers out and tosses one to Liam.

"I'll try to get more later," I say. "Soon enough they'll all be drunk and won't even know we're in the house."

"That's what I'm counting on," Liam says as he makes a crude 'fucking' gesture, thrusting his hips back and forth as he gazes at Luanne. Charming.

"I always know you're in the room," Caleb says, his voice lower, full of heat as he grabs me. He pulls me to him and his cock presses against my stomach. Heat sizzles through me, but it's not from Caleb. Nope, not from Caleb at all. I angle my head, catch Jack watching us. I should push Caleb away. I want Jack to know I'm his and his alone, but it's so hard waiting. Instead of shoving the slimeball asshole off me, I put my hands on his chest and laugh. I can feel Jack's rage through the glass patio doors. I shouldn't poke him so hard, but when it comes time for him to take me, I don't want him holding back an inch. I want him to let his guard down, to use and abuse my body the way he needs. The way we both need.

"Caleb, you're such a pig," I say, then break from the circle of his arms. "Find us something to watch. I need to shower. Some of us do work during the day, you know."

"Need any help up there?" Caleb asks, ignoring my jibe about him lounging all summer while the rest of us work to pay for college. He comes from money, I don't. Even if I did, I doubt my parents would help me. They didn't want me in the first place. Guilt for being alive and interfering with their hopes and dreams tangles in my gut. Both my mom and dad planned to become lawyers, but instead my mom now works retail and my dad became a cop. They make a descent living, but constantly remind me they could have done better, had they not made a 'mistake' with me.

Not wanting to think about the disappointment my life has brought them, I say, "I think I know how to get all those hard to reach places myself. I've been touching them myself for quite some time."

"If you tease me like that, you're going to get what you deserve." There is a warning edge to his voice, and it actually makes me a bit nervous as I bolt up the stairs. I really don't know Caleb that well. I only started hanging out with him a few weeks ago when Luanne hooked up with his best friend, Liam.

I strip off the god-awful brown uniform I have to wear in the food court, drop my phone onto the counter and turn the water on hot. I open the sliding glass door and stand under the spray. As it pours over my naked body, I exhale a soft breath and grab my favorite vanilla-scented soap to lather up. My hands skim my body and the whole time I picture Jack in the shower with me, his mouth all over me, between my needy legs, licking and sucking and taking what's his. I continue to pleasure myself, my mind on an erotic journey as bubbles form in my hands. A soft moan escapes my throat, my clit so swollen I'm only seconds away from an orgasm.

"Is that moan for me?" I hear from the other side of the glass shower door, and gasp when I turn to see Caleb standing in the bathroom.

"Get out of here," I say, and cover my body with my hands.

"You know you don't want that. Let me come in there with you, show you how good I can make you feel."

"I'll scream."

He laughs. "Everyone is shit-faced drunk." He pops the button on his pants, and panic explodes inside me. "Go ahead and scream. No one's going to hear you."

"I'll hear her."

At the sound of Jack's voice, my heart jumps into my throat. Through the steam, I see Jack's big outline as he steps into the room and stands over Caleb. God, he's so huge and intimidating, if I didn't know him, I'd be shaking in my boots.

"Hey come on. She invited me."

Jack looks at me, and even through the mist, his eyes are piercing and deadly as they meet mine. "Is that true?"

"No," I say without hesitation, my pulse pounding so hard in my neck the room grows fuzzy.

Guard up, jaw tight, Jack turns his focus back to Caleb. Caleb snorts and says, "I'm a minor. Lay one hand on me and you'll be in a shitload of trouble, pal."

I've never seen Jack wound so tight. His gaze is focused, targeted, with Caleb smack-dab in the crosshairs. "Lay one hand on her and same goes for you, pal."

Caleb stands there for a moment, sizing up his opponent like he's actually thinking about taking him on. The guy clearly isn't too bright. Then, as if deciding it's a suicide mission, he backs down, and lowers his gaze. "Fine. I'm fucking leaving. No piece of ass is worth the trouble."

Jack's eyes narrow in anger, and his fingers curl into fists like something has been unleashed inside him. I don't think he's going to attack Caleb—as much as he looks like he wants to. The fight wouldn't be fair, and if there is one thing I know about Jack, he's a just and ethical man—a real rule follower. He's a man of his word, and when he makes a promise, he sticks to it.

"Don't go near her again. Ever," he seethes. "I'll be watching and if you do, I won't let you walk away in one piece next time."

Jack turns to the side to let Caleb pass. Caleb looks like he's about to pee his pants, but once he clears Jack, he seems to gather an ounce of bravado, and shoots back with, "What is she to you anyway?"

I slide the humid glass panel open, and steam billows into the room. Jack has his back to me—clearly glaring at Caleb—but I'm sure I heard him say, "Everything," under his breath as Caleb rushes down the stairs.

"Thanks, Jack," I say and fight off a tremble. I hate to think what could have happened if he hadn't shown up. "I guess you were right about him."

His body is rigid, his back hard, and I wish I could wrap my arms around him, hold him tight and help loosen him up a bit. "I'm right about a lot of things," he murmurs.

"I know," I say in total agreement. I trust Jack, trust and take everything he says to heart.

"I don't think he'll be bothering you again."

I grab a towel off the hook and wrap myself in it. "You can turn around. I'm covered."

He turns, and takes in the big fluffy towel as I knot it over my breasts. I draw in a slow breath, everything about this man seducing my senses.

"Where's your phone?" He scrubs his face like he's in total agony. I gesture to the bathroom counter. He picks it up and swipes a big finger over the screen. God, how I want those fingers on my body, deep between my legs. My clit throbs and I squeeze my thighs together, desperate for an orgasm.

"I'm punching my number in." Rich, intense eyes lock on mine as he breathes in, the scent of my vanilla soap strong in the room. "If you ever find yourself in trouble and need anything, don't hesitate to call. If you're in a situation where you can't call, text with the word 'vanilla.' It will be inconspicuous to others, but I'll know you need me."

My heart thumps at how sweet he is. "You're giving me a safe word?"

He angles his head, gives me a dark, warning look that I

totally recognize. He hates the thought of me with anyone else, as much as I hate the thought of him with some other woman.

"What do you know about safe words, Layla?"

I grin. "Oh, not much. Just what I've read. But when I'm with you, you can bet you'll never hear the word *vanilla* come out of my mouth," I say. His turbulent gaze alerts me to the fact that he gets the meaning behind my words—when it comes to him, vanilla is the last thing I want. I look him over; the need to hand myself to him, let him take charge of my body is so intense it's almost painful. I put my palm on his bare chest, feel the strength of his heartbeat beneath my fingers.

"You don't need to say it, just text it when you need something," he says.

"There *is* something I need, Jack."

"What...what do you need?" he asks, his eyes half closed, like he's in total agony. God, he's so intense, so unlike the boring guys from my school.

"I need you." His lids flash open and I give him a small smile as I shake my wet hair out. It falls over my back, and my breath comes out in a low hush when I say, "But you already know that."

Desire clouds his eyes. "You can't have me."

"Not yet, but soon," I say, playing by society's rules for a little bit longer. "While I'm waiting, I just need something to help me get through the next few weeks." I drop my towel and expose my naked, quivering body.

His gaze rakes over me. Hungry. Ravenous. Dangerous. "You're so fucking beautiful," he murmurs.

"And I'm all yours."

His eyes glaze, like he's forgotten all rational thought, but then a laugh sounds outside my window. A splash follows the sound as some other drunken cop lands in the pool.

"Layla, fuck..." The sound pulls him back and he inches away.

I step up to him again, push against his thigh and he holds his hands up, palms out. "I can't touch you. I won't."

He's such a good man and that's one of the reasons I love him. "Then don't," I say, never wanting to get him into any kind of trouble. "Don't touch me, Jack. Just stand here, hands behind your back."

I shove his hands around his body, and as I do, I straddle his leg, and push down until my hot sex is wide open on his bare thigh.

He sucks in a quick breath. "Holy fuck."

I move against him, rub my clit, and let loose a low, needy moan. I know he's currently off limits—sex with him taboo— but everything about this feels so good, so right. As heat zings through my body, I cup my breasts, needing something to do with my hands before I run them all over his hard muscles.

"You're so wet," he murmurs going as still as a stealth soldier as I continue to rock against him. I move restlessly and my clit swells, still so achy and needy from not being able to finish myself off in the shower.

His gaze slides over me, then he pinches his eyes tight shut. "This is so wrong."

"You're not doing anything wrong, Jack. And for me, it feels so right." I press down harder, and heat sparks through me as I ride his leg, taking what I need from him, for the time being.

"I'm going to come all over your legs," I say.

"You're going to be the death of me," he growls and links his hands behind his neck.

I chuckle. "Just think, in a couple of weeks, you're going to be able to do anything you want to me. Anything at all. I won't say no to you, Jack. I won't say no to anything."

"Jesus, fuck," he growls, as I pick up speed.

"Then after college, we can move away, finally get out of Texas like we both want. You have that job in New York you're always talking about, and once I have my law degree, there will be plenty of firms where I can work."

As I think about the life we can have together, I rub myself hard, creating friction as I massage my breasts. I throw my head back and punch my nipples until they're swollen and begging for this man's hot mouth.

"In a few weeks, when I'm finally allowed, I'm going to take your cock into my mouth. I want to swallow every inch of you. You'll let me do that won't you, Jack? You'll let me take your cock so deep into my throat that I won't be able to breathe."

He grunts in response, the sound so loaded with promise it makes me a little hotter and a whole lot wetter. My lids flutter, and I angle my head to see the agony he's in as his cock throbs, but I won't touch him. I'm not allowed.

"I'm going to want you to own me, everywhere. Nothing is off limits. You can own my mouth, my pussy, and my ass."

"I'm going to fucking own you, Layla."

A hard quiver moves through me at the deepness of his voice. I hate that I can't help him take the edge off. But I'm not going to break his no touching rule. Than again, I guess I sort of am by rubbing my pussy on his leg. At least our hands aren't involved, which is his hard rule. I gyrate, and slide over his muscular thigh, taking what I need. Each movement builds heat and friction, and in no time at all an explosion tears through me. My body soars, each clench taking me higher and higher until I'm free-falling without a net.

"Jesus Christ," he groans as I soak his leg, my juices dripping down his thigh.

God, if this is what can happen when he doesn't even touch me, I can't imagine what will happen to me when he finally does. I take deep gulping breaths, and Jack stays still, his eyes holding my gaze as my heartbeat regulates and I come back down to earth.

"I have to go," he murmurs, once my body has settled again.

"I know." He inches back, and a burst of cool air brushes over my body with his absence. My pussy aches for him as he grabs my towel off the floor and wraps me in it. His hands are big and rough, but so gentle on my body. "I'll see you soon, Jack," I say, my voice full of promise.

"Don't forget your safe word, Layla," he responds.

"Will you come running to me like a knight in shining armor?" I ask.

He grins, and turns his back on me. I watch him go, and my body quivers as I mentally count down the days until the time is right, and he can finally be mine.

ABOUT CATHRYN

New York Times and *USA today* Bestselling author, Cathryn is a wife, mom, sister, daughter, and friend. She loves dogs, sunny weather, anything chocolate (she never says no to a brownie) pizza and red wine. She has two teenagers who keep her busy with their never ending activities, and a husband who is convinced he can turn her into a mixed martial arts fan. Cathryn can never find balance in her life, is always trying to find time to go to the gym, can never keep up with emails, Facebook or Twitter and tries to write page-turning books that her readers will love.

Connect with Cathryn:
Newsletter
https://app.mailerlite.com/webforms/landing/c1f8n1
Twitter: https://twitter.com/writercatfox
Facebook:
https://www.facebook.com/AuthorCathrynFox?ref=hl
Blog: http://cathrynfox.com/blog/

Goodreads:
https://www.goodreads.com/author/show/91799.Cathryn_Fox
Pinterest http://www.pinterest.com/catkalen/

House Rules

Boys of Beachville
Good at Being Bad
Igniting the Bad Boy
Bad Girl Therapy

Stone Cliff Series:
Crashing Down
Wasted Summer
Love Lessons
Wrapped Up

Eternal Pleasure Series
Instinctive
Impulsive
Indulgent

Sun Stroked Series
Seaside Seduction
Deep Desire
Private Pleasure

Captured and Claimed Series:
Yours to Take
Yours to Teach
Yours to Keep

Firefighter Heat Series

Fever

Siren

Flash Fire

Playing For Keeps Series

Slow Ride

Wild Ride

Sweet Ride

Breaking the Rules:

Hold Me Down Hard

Pin Me Up Proper

Tie Me Down Tight

Stand Alone Title:

Hands on with the CEO

Torn Between Two Brothers

Holiday Spirit

Unleashed

Knocking on Demon's Door

Web of Desire